"Do you want to leave, Leah?"

Paul asked.

"No..." Leah's eyes were dewy and defiant. "But it seems...above and beyond the call of duty for you to have to marry me. I've already explained that I'm not the marrying kind."

His eyes narrowed. "I never have understood that attitude. You're a warm, generous woman. What makes you think you're so unmarriable?"

She hesitated, her heart racing with hope. "Are—are you saying you'd be willing to marry me?"

"Yes," he told her. "If it wasn't so unfair to you."

"Unfair?"

"Leah, I'm raising three motherless children. And...I don't have anything to offer you."

"What about children I love?" Leah demanded. "A home and a family."

His gaze connected with hers. "That would be enough for you?"

She nodded.

"Will you marry me, Leah," he asked in a voice gruff with emotion, "for all our sakes?"

"Yes," she whispered, "I'll marry you."

Dear Reader,

Welcome to Silhouette **Special Edition** . . . welcome to romance. Each month, Silhouette **Special Edition** publishes six novels with you in mind—stories of love and life, tales that you can identify with—romance with that little "something special" added in.

May has some wonderful stories blossoming for you. Don't miss Debbie Macomber's continuing series, THOSE MANNING MEN. This month, we're pleased to present *Stand-in Wife,* Paul and Leah's story. And starting this month is Myrna Temte's new series, COWBOY COUNTRY. *For Pete's Sake* is set in Wyoming and should delight anyone who enjoys the classic ranch story.

Rounding out this month are more stories by some of your favorite authors: Lisa Jackson, Ruth Wind, Andrea Edwards. And say hello to Kari Sutherland. Her debut book, *Wish on the Moon,* is also coming your way this month.

In each Silhouette **Special Edition** novel, we're dedicated to bringing you the romances that you dream about—stories that will delight as well as bring a tear to the eye. And that's what Silhouette **Special Edition** is all about—special books by special authors for special readers!

I hope you enjoy this book and all of the stories to come!

Sincerely,

Tara Gavin
Senior Editor
Silhouette Books

DEBBIE MACOMBER
Stand-in Wife

Silhouette Special Edition

Published by Silhouette Books New York

America's Publisher of Contemporary Romance

Dedicated to Lucy Beckstead
Thank you for showing me the way,
then taking me by the hand and guiding me there

In Memory of Kim Gonzalez;
and for Tyler, who will never know his mother

SILHOUETTE BOOKS
300 East 42nd St., New York, N.Y. 10017

STAND-IN WIFE

ISBN: 0-373-09744-1

First Silhouette Books printing May 1992

Books by Debbie Macomber

DEBBIE MACOMBER

hails from the state of Washington. As a busy wife and mother of four, she strives to keep her family healthy and happy. As the prolific author of dozens of best-selling romance novels, she strives to keep her readers happy with each new book she writes.

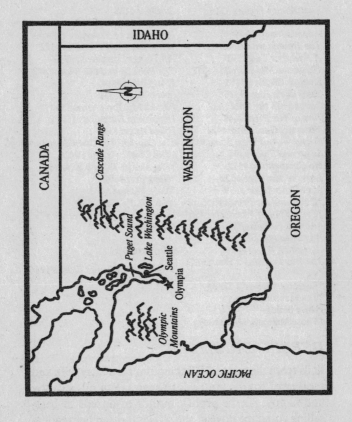

Prologue

The morning was bleak; the sky, gray and overcast. The phone call from the hospital had woken Paul Manning from a sound slumber, his first decent sleep since his daughter Kelsey Diane had been born seventy-two hours earlier. Because of the problem with toxemia, his wife, Diane, had been placed in the intensive care unit as a precaution.

Matters, however, had quickly gone bad, complicated by the fact that Diane had been born with only one kidney. Generally the toxins disappeared from the mother's body following birth, but in Diane's case that hadn't happened. Instead they'd attacked her liver and lone kidney, and before Paul fully realized the seriousness of her condition, she'd quietly slipped into a coma. Paul and Diane's sister, Leah, had held a vigil at her side. After two days Dr. Charman had sent them home, promising to contact Paul if there was any change. Now he was proving true to his word.

"Could you come to the hospital?"

"What's wrong?" Paul demanded, hearing the weary frustration in the physician's voice.

"It'd be best if you came to the hospital. I'll explain everything once you're here."

It wasn't supposed to happen like this.

A half hour later Paul Manning was shouting the words in his mind, but not a sound passed from his lips. The powerful fists of pain, disbelief and shock viciously punched at him, knocking the wind from his lungs. Feeling dizzy and weak, he slumped into the molded plastic hospital chair.

"We did everything we could," Dr. Charman murmured, his voice subdued with defeat.

Women gave birth...but they didn't die from it. Not in this day and age. Not when they were in one of the best medical facilities in the country.

The pregnancy had started out routine. Diane had never seemed healthier. Then, in the eighth month of her pregnancy she'd developed toxemia. Paul hadn't been overly concerned, blithely unaware of how deadly her condition would prove to be.

Diane had suffered the same malady during her first pregnancy, and everything had turned out all right. The twins had been born six weeks prematurely, but the effects of toxemia hadn't been life threatening to either her or the boys.

"Is there someone you'd like me to call?"

Paul glanced up and shook his head. He didn't want his family just yet. For now he needed to grieve alone. "I'd like to be with her for a few minutes if I could."

Dr. Charman nodded and led the way down the quiet corridor to Diane's room. Paul's heart was pounding savagely, his head whirling, his legs unsteady. He felt as though he were walking in a nightmare, and he prayed someone would mercifully shake him awake.

Dr. Charman opened the door and stepped aside. "I'll wait for you here," he said.

Paul nodded, surprised by the calm that enveloped him. He hadn't expected to feel serenity. Not when the grief, guilt and pain were crushing his heart.

The first thing he noticed was that all the tubes had been disconnected. His wife's face was aglow with a beauty that transcended anything he'd ever known. Serene and peaceful. For a moment he was sure Dr. Charman had made a mistake, that Diane was only sleeping.

He remembered the first time he'd met Diane six years earlier. He had been in the army, stationed in Alaska, and she'd come up to work for the summer in a cannery. He was nearly thirty and she was barely twenty-one. Paul had taken one look at her with her free-flowing beauty, and his heart had stopped. He'd fallen in love a dozen times, but no woman had ever affected him the way Diane Baker had. By the end of the summer he'd convinced her to drop out of college and marry him.

They'd talked for hours on end, plotting their future. Paul's degree was in journalism, but one day he intended to be a novelist. Diane had read his work, built up his confidence, convinced him the time would come when he would sell his stories. Through the years her belief in him remained unwavering.

Within six months after they were married she was pregnant. When she delivered Ryan and Ronnie, Paul thought his heart would burst with pride. Twin sons.

Then, a year ago Diane had decided she wanted a little girl. Paul would have preferred to have waited, spaced out their family, gotten the boys in school first. But Diane had been adamant. She'd wanted another baby. They'd argued about it, but in the end she'd convinced him. Actually it was a sheer black nightie that had finally persuaded him. He never had been able to refuse his wife. She was his whole world and now she was gone.

Paul looked down at her, and his heart felt heavy and empty. It was as if she'd taken his life with her. What would he do without Diane? How could he possibly face life without her at his side?

Diane was at peace, but Paul's heart was in turmoil.

Pain clawed at his chest, and the knot built up in his throat until a sliver of the anguish escaped in a low moan. Gripping the raised railing of the hospital bed, he closed his eyes and felt his body rock with grief.

The sounds outside the room caught his attention and he turned, recognizing a voice that belonged to Leah, Diane's sister.

The two women had always been close, and it didn't surprise him that she was there. Moving from his wife's side, he opened the door to find a stricken Leah pleading with Dr. Charman.

"Paul?" She'd shifted her imploring gaze to him. "I woke...something told me to come to the hospital...right then...not to wait. I'd only been home a few hours."

Paul nodded. He hadn't been asleep long himself.

"I can't believe this is happening," she sobbed. "Not to Diane..." She placed her hand over her mouth, and her shoulders shook with the pain of loss that went soul deep.

Paul held his arms open to her, and Leah walked into his embrace, but he didn't know who was comforting whom.

He needed her and she needed him.

Chapter One

The weak cry from Kelsey stirred Paul from his light sleep. He blinked a couple of times and rubbed a hand down his weary face. The midnight feedings were the worst, especially those on Friday night.

Life had fallen into a dismal pattern since Diane's funeral. He'd never worked harder in his life than in the past six months. Keeping up with the kids and the house and his job left room for little else. The demands seemed endless.

His family had pitched in to help in every way they could. Between his mother and his sister-in-law he was making it.

Just barely.

Kelsey squalled again, and Paul tossed aside the covers and sat on the edge of the mattress. Blindly he searched with his feet for his slippers before he stood and slipped into his robe.

Kelsey slept in the crib in his room, and he automatically reached for her, gently placing his infant daughter over his shoulder.

"Just a minute, sweetheart," he said, walking in a circle around the room until he'd located a freshly laundered diaper on top of the dresser.

Bless Leah. He didn't know what he'd do if she hadn't taken over the laundry. With so many extra medical expenses, plus the cost of the funeral, he couldn't afford a diaper service or even disposables. So every afternoon on her way home from teaching at the college, Leah stopped in to prepare dinner and start the washing machine. Paul didn't know how he'd have survived the past few months without the help of Leah and his mother.

With an expert hand he deftly changed Kelsey's wet diaper while her bottle was heating in the microwave. He was getting fairly good at this diapering business. Early in his married life, Paul had teased Diane that she could have as many children as she wanted as long as she was the one who dealt with the messy diapers. Now changing diapers, like so many other tasks, had become his job alone.

Settling down with Kelsey in the rocking chair in the living room, Paul carefully placed the rubber nipple against her lips. The baby's tiny mouth parted, and she sucked hungrily.

His hand brushed the soft blond wisps of hair from her sweet face. How grateful he was that Kelsey had been born healthy. Diane had wanted a little girl so badly. They'd learned early in the pregnancy, through an ultrasound test, that his wife was to have her wish. Paul hadn't cared one way or the other, but Diane had been overjoyed at the prospect of a daughter.

Paul had been in the delivery room when Kelsey had been born. Because there had been so much concern about Diane's condition, they'd handed Kelsey to him. Even now, six months later, he remembered the surge of love and pride he'd experienced holding his newborn daughter that first time.

It wasn't Kelsey's fault that her birth had cost Diane her life. Not once had Paul thought to place blame. Who was there to accuse? God? Fate? Life?

Paul didn't know. He'd given up looking for a scapegoat. There wasn't enough time or energy left in a day. Not when he had to deal with the reality of raising three motherless children, age four and under.

Once Kelsey had finished the bottle, Paul placed her over his shoulder and tenderly rubbed her back. Gently rocking back and forth, he closed his eyes. He'd rest for just a moment . . . he promised himself.

For just a moment . . .

Leah let herself in the house that had once been her sister's to find her brother-in-law asleep in the rocking chair, his arms gently cradling Kelsey.

She hesitated, not wanting to disturb him. He'd looked so tired lately. They both had.

Too tired to grieve.

Too tired to do anything more than function, taking one step at a time, dragging one day into the next. Moving forward, because they had no choice.

Even now, several months after her sister's death, Leah had trouble accepting the permanence of the situation. More times than she could count, Leah expected Diane to come waltzing into the room with her warm smile and bubbly personality. How empty life felt without her. It was as though a giant black hole had been created by her death.

She felt it.

Paul felt it.

The children felt it, too.

Then some days it was as if Diane actually were there with Leah and Paul. At the oddest times Leah felt as though her sister were standing at her side, thanking her for helping, for encouraging Paul.

And then there was the dream.

Leah had never told her brother-in-law about it. She'd never told anyone. It had come the night Diane had died.

Paul and Leah had been at the hospital with her sister three days, and there hadn't been any change in Diane's condition for several hours. Dr. Charman had insisted they both go home and get some decent sleep. Nothing was likely to happen for some time yet. Paul had been as reluctant about leaving as Leah had been, but in the end they'd both finally agreed.

Leah had walked into her apartment, showered and gone to bed. The instant her head had hit the pillow she'd fallen into a deep sleep. In her dream Diane had come to her, walking toward her in a fresh field of blooming wildflowers. She was barefoot and happy, chasing butterflies. Then she'd relaxed under a flowering magnolia tree and smiled at Leah. A brilliant white light had come and settled above her. Diane had paused and smiled into the light, and although Leah couldn't hear what her sister was saying, it had seemed to her that Diane was requesting a few more minutes. Apparently she got what she wanted. She had turned from the radiant light and looked again to Leah.

Holding a daisy in her hand and plucking at the petals, she had told Leah how sorry she was to leave her, Paul and the children. Leah had tried to interrupt, but Diane had stopped her. Her sister had gone on to explain how hard she'd battled to live, but was beginning to understand that there was a greater wisdom in her going. She'd come to accept that.

The problem, she explained, was that she couldn't freely give up her life with both Paul and Leah at the hospital. The strength of their love and their will physically held on to her, prevented her from dying. It was the reason they'd been sent home. Once they were gone, she would be free.

Again Leah had tried to argue with her, but Diane had smiled serenely and silenced her, claiming there wasn't enough time. She had spoken quickly, pointing out to Leah that Paul and the children would need her help. She'd hesitated and after a moment looked directly into Leah's eyes. She had smiled and then asked if Leah would be willing to take her place. Leah hadn't understood then and she wasn't completely sure she did even now, but in the end she'd promised her sister she'd do whatever was needed.

In the next instant Leah had woken. For a confused moment she had remained in bed, certain it had all been a dream, a figment of her imagination. Diane *was* at the hospital and it *was* true, her condition was listed as serious, but her sister *wasn't* going to die. No one had even mentioned the possibility of Diane dying. Quickly Leah had gotten out of bed and rushed back to the hospital only to discover Paul was already there with Dr. Charman.

Her sister was gone.

The dream had haunted Leah for months. She'd kept her promise to Diane and was doing everything she possibly could to help Paul with the children, but it seemed so little.

To his credit, Paul was holding up well. He was such a good father. But frankly Leah wondered just how much longer he would be able to continue under the strain. He'd been the strong one, reassuring her, reassuring his children, his parents and everyone else. Strong and capable.

Leah didn't know how he did it. But she was grateful. His confidence was the glue that had held everything together. Leah wasn't the only one who was helping. Paul's mother took in the children during the day for him. The cost of day care for three preschoolers was outrageous. When Paul told her the quotes he'd gotten from several child-care facilities, she'd thought he was joking. He couldn't survive financially paying those fees.

Because Paul's hours at the newspaper often stretched past six o'clock, Leah had gotten into the habit of picking up the boys and Kelsey at his mother's place on her way home from the college where she taught. Since the kids were usually hungry, she'd start dinner then. She'd also run a load or two of laundry and do whatever else she could to lighten Paul's obligations.

For six months they'd all worked together, doing what they could. Leah, however, was growing concerned. Elizabeth Manning was a wonderful woman, but it had been a long time since she'd been responsible for small children, and the demands of caring for three of them were beginning to take their toll. For nearly a year the older Mannings had been planning a trip to Montana to visit Paul's two sisters. Christy was pregnant with her first child, and Elizabeth Manning was hoping to be with her youngest daughter for the birth of her fifth grandchild.

Paul was as concerned about the situation as Leah was. Even more so. She hadn't a clue of what he intended to do. The problem was, Paul probably didn't have one, either.

What the hell could he do?

"Mommy." Four-year-old Ryan, the older of the identical twins, came out from the bedroom, sleepily rubbing his eyes. He dragged his security blanket on the carpet behind him.

"Good morning, sweetheart," Leah said, automatically lifting the warm, cuddly body into her arms.

"I want my mommy." Ryan's arms tightly gripped her as he buried his face in Leah's neck.

"I know." Her heart caught on his words.

"When will she be home?"

"Your mommy's in heaven now, remember?"

"But when will she come back?"

Unexpected tears filled Leah's eyes. "She won't... don't you remember what your daddy said?"

"But I want her to."

"I do, too." It was difficult to make Ryan and Ronnie understand, difficult to understand herself. And it didn't seem to be getting any easier.

If death had to steal a life, then it should have been her the Grim Reaper had sought. Diane had had a husband, children, responsibilities. Her sister had been gentle and sweet, full of life and laughter. It made no sense to Leah. None. Diane had always been blond and pretty, animated and energetic. Leah was tall and ungainly. At five eight she was a full five inches taller than her younger sister. Her hair was a pale shade of brown, and her eyes an indeterminate color, a cross between green and brown depending on what she chose to wear. Diane had been the striking one in the family.

Diane had been the only family Leah had. Their parents had divorced when they were young, and their mother had died several years back. They'd lost contact with their father in their youth. Now Diane's grieving children were Leah's only family.

"Are you hungry?" Leah asked Ryan, turning the conversation away from the painful subject of Diane.

Ryan's head was buried in her shoulder. He sniffled and nodded. "Can you make Egg McManning the way Mommy did?"

"Ah..." Leah hesitated. She hadn't a clue what Egg McManning was. "Sure, but you'll have to show me how."

"Okay." Ryan brightened a little. "First you cook eggs and cheese and muffins, and then you put everything together and eat it."

"Ah..." Once again Leah hesitated. She was going to need a few more instructions than that. Diane had had an active imagination. She could make the most mundane chores fun and the simplest meal a feast.

"I'm hungry." Ronnie traipsed out of his bedroom and into the kitchen. Using both hands, he scooted out the kitchen chair, then curled up into a ball on the seat. He stuck his thumb in his mouth.

"Aunt Leah's making Egg McManning," Ryan told him.

"Good." The thumb was in and out of his mouth long enough to say the single word.

Until Diane's death Ronnie had given up sucking his thumb, but he seemed to need it lately. Leah hadn't suggested he stop and wouldn't for a while. Life had already thrown the little boy one harsh blow; she wasn't about to chastise him because he needed a little extra security.

"Did I hear someone mention serving Egg Mc-Manning for breakfast?" Paul stood in the kitchen doorway. Kelsey remained on his shoulder, sleeping soundly.

"Aunt Leah's cooking them for us," Ryan explained cheerfully.

"I hope you're up to sharing the recipe with me," she muttered under her breath.

"Toast English muffins," Paul instructed between yawns, "add a scrambled egg, a slice of cheese and voilà." He pressed the back of his hand to his mouth and yawned loudly. "How long have you been here?"

"Only a few minutes." Leah had her back to him, searching the contents of the refrigerator for a carton of eggs.

"I thought you couldn't come until noon."

"I lied," she tossed gingerly over her shoulder. "I spruced up my place last night and figured I'd get a head start this morning with the kids." She set the eggs, muffins and cheese on the kitchen counter. "I thought Ryan and Ronnie might enjoy a trip to the zoo." Out of the corner of her eye she watched for the twins' re-action.

"The zoo?" Ronnie asked excitedly. "With lions and tigers and bears?"

"I thought you had a date last night?" Paul asked, frowning.

"I was too tired to go out." She found a skillet that had been left to dry in the rack next to the sink and set it on top of the stove.

"If you were so tired, where'd you find the energy to clean house?"

Paul was like that sometimes, Leah noted. She guessed it was the reporter in him. He'd prod until he got the answer he already knew to be the truth.

"If I were you," she said, waving a spatula in his direction, "I wouldn't look a gift horse in the mouth."

"I know what you're doing." Fierce pride bright-ened his blue eyes.

"So do I," she countered smoothly. "I'm cooking breakfast for two hungry little boys."

Kelsey woke and started fussing. Paul looked as if he'd prefer to continue their conversation, but didn't know which to do first, deal with his daughter or with Leah.

"I'll heat her bottle for you," she offered, cutting off his reply before he could make it.

Paul looked haggard. She'd purposely stopped off early so he could have a portion of the day to himself. The guy was running himself ragged. They all were. But for Leah there was an escape. At the end of the day she returned to her own apartment, free from the de-mands of three small, needy children. A place of her own where she could find a few moments' peace and serenity. Paul had no such deliverance.

Breakfast was ready by the time Paul returned with a freshly diapered Kelsey. He'd taken the time to dress in jeans and a sweatshirt himself. Leah did little more than glance in his direction.

She set three plates on the table and automatically reached for Kelsey, tucking the baby in her arms and smiling softly as the infant eagerly took to the warm milk.

"You're ruining your social life," Paul said, biting into the muffin as though it had been several days since his last decent meal.

"I'm not." There wasn't a social life to ruin, Leah thought. She only dated occasionally. Bill was a friend and would never be anything more. They generally had a good time together, but canceling an evening with him wasn't the end of the world.

"You should have gone out last night."

"I wasn't in the mood." Gently she rubbed her hand along the side of Kelsey's angelic face, her heart constricting as she noted the resemblance the little one already had to Diane.

"Leah, please don't."

The earnestness in Paul's voice captured her attention. Slowly she lifted her gaze to his.

"I feel guilty enough knowing what this is doing to my parents," he said, his eyes holding hers captive. "Please don't sacrifice yourself for me, too."

"It's not for you," she countered smoothly. "It's for Ryan, Ronnie and Kelsey. And it isn't a sacrifice. If the situation were reversed, Diane wouldn't think twice about doing the same for me. It's what she expected."

Paul closed his eyes and nodded, his face grim. "I don't feel good about it."

"I know." Leah did know. It went against Paul's pride to rely on his family so heavily. He didn't have any choice, but he didn't like it.

Not one bit.

Paul was in an angry, unreasonable mood. He found himself short-tempered and cross. If there was anything to be grateful for, it was that Leah had taken the boys to the zoo and Kelsey was napping.

He would have liked nothing more than to sit down and relax at his computer. He was five chapters into a book, but he hadn't written a word since Diane's death. How could he? There hadn't been a spare moment he could call his own. If he'd had any extra time at all, he would have joined his two younger brothers when they'd asked him to become part of their softball team. He felt a bit guilty for spurning Jason and Rich's efforts to help, but feeling like a charity case was worse.

There wouldn't have been time for softball this Saturday anyway, since a dozen chores or more needed to be done around the house. It wasn't any different than any other weekend, and yet it was.

One of the twins had pulled the towel rack off the bathroom wall. When he'd asked who was responsible, both Ryan and Ronnie had claimed, "not me." *Not me* seemed to have a lot to answer for, lately.

Once he finished the bathroom, Paul moved into the twins' bedroom where the closet door was off the track. It wasn't a simple task setting it back into place. Again and again he had to struggle to fit it onto the narrow groove until it was all he could do not to rip the door out completely in his frustration.

"You're losing it, old boy," he said, forcing himself to step back and suck in several deep, calming breaths.

From there, Paul moved to the garage. His car needed an oil change, and although he'd gotten in the habit of having it done at a twenty-minute lube place, this time he opted to do the task himself, hoping to save a few dollars.

Tinkering around the garage, he decided to run to the hardware store for a few items. No big deal. He'd be back in fifteen, twenty minutes tops. It wasn't until he was a block down the road that he remembered Kelsey.

He tore back to the house like a madman and raced inside the front door, his heart pounding like a piston against his ribs—so hard and loud it sounded like thunder in his ear.

Kelsey was sleeping soundly, completely unaware that her own father had so thoughtlessly left her behind.

Slumping into the rocking chair, Paul rammed his fingers through his hair. He clenched his fist at his side, resisting the urge to plow it through the wall. Paul had never been a violent man, and the rage that surged through him took him by storm. If it wasn't a fist against the wall, it was one raised in abject frustration at the heavens for dealing him such a cruel fate.

Leah's timing couldn't have been worse. The boys exploded through the front door, happy and excited. Ryan and Ronnie were each clenching a bright red balloon in one hand and an ice-cream cone in the other.

"Daddy, Daddy, guess what we saw?"

Paul didn't answer, but that didn't seem to dampen Ryan's enthusiasm.

"There was an eagle, a great big one with wings as long as an airplane and huge claws." He formed his small hand into the shape. "Bigger even than this."

"Paul, what's wrong?" Leah's gentle voice came to him, soft and serene. If he were to close his eyes, he could almost believe it was Diane speaking to him— only it wasn't Diane, and he knew it.

"I left the house to do one small errand."

"Yes?"

She didn't seem to understand. "I went without Kelsey. I left her in the house alone," he said, his voice raised. "Anything could have happened, don't you understand? I left my own daughter...I completely forgot about her."

"Nothing happened. It's not the end of the world."

"Isn't it?" he shouted.

Leah placed one hand around each boy's shoulder and steered them toward the kitchen. "Finish your cones at the table and then wash your hands," she told them calmly, evenly. "Then it's time for your nap."

"Ronnie, get your thumb out of your mouth," Paul flared. "You're too old to be sucking your thumb."

The boy raised stricken eyes toward his father, and rushed into the other room.

"Take a few minutes to relax," Leah instructed, "and I'll bring you a cup of tea."

"I don't want any damn tea."

"I know," she answered. "You want Diane back. We all do."

"A cup of tea isn't going to help."

"Perhaps not, but we need to talk, and any time Diane had something important she wanted to discuss, she did it over a cup of tea."

Paul didn't need his sister-in-law to tell him about his dead wife's habits. For an instant he wanted to lash out at her, the same way he'd lashed out at Ronnie. But the guilt he felt at his unreasonable anger compounded as he followed Leah into the kitchen. Ryan and Ronnie were sitting at the table. Their happy excitement was gone, their young shoulders hunched forward. Paul leaned over and kissed Ronnie's cheek. "I'm sorry I snapped at you."

"I won't suck my thumb anymore," the four-year-old promised.

Ryan scooted off the chair and raced toward his bedroom, returning with his yellow blanket which he indignantly handed Paul. "If Ronnie can't have his thumb, then I don't want my blankie."

"You're sure?" Paul asked. Ryan hadn't slept without his blanket since Diane's death.

"Yes," his son informed him with a hard shake of his head.

"If you're finished, go wash your hands," Leah told the boys. "It's time for your nap."

Paul expected an argument. The boys rarely went to sleep without a fuss these days. They seemed to feel that if they were old enough for kindergarten in September then they were much too old for afternoon naps. To his surprise neither one voiced a word of protest.

He was left alone as Leah walked down the hallway with the boys. She returned a couple of minutes later and poured them both a cup of hot tea.

She was about to sit down when Ryan walked into the kitchen, braced his feet apart and glared toward his father. Paul wasn't surprised. Here it comes, he thought. The argument against naptime.

"What is it?" Paul demanded impatiently.

Ryan blinked, looked to the blanket piled on the chair next to Paul. "Ronnie's got his thumb back so I want my blankie." With that he scooped up the tattered yellow monstrosity and raced back into his bedroom.

Leah was smiling, and if he'd been in any better mood, Paul would have found humor in it, too.

"So you had a good time at the zoo?"

"Yes. The boys were great." Her hands framed the delicate teacup as though she was seeking a way to warm her hands. "Listen, Paul, I've been doing some thinking about the situation here with you and the kids, and it seems to me we need to come up with some solutions."

"We? This isn't your problem."

"Yes it is, although I hesitate to call it a problem."

"Then what the hell would you call it?"

"An opportunity."

"An opportunity for what?" he demanded, hating the way he raised his voice. The anger he felt simmered just below the surface, and seemed ready to explode at the slightest provocation.

"I've given a lot of thought to what I'm about to propose."

"Leah, listen, forgive me, I'm in a foul mood and not good company. I don't know what's wrong with me, but I—"

"I know what's wrong. What's wrong with all of us. Why Ronnie's started sucking his thumb again and why Ryan can't get to sleep unless he's got his blankie with him."

"It's Diane..."

"We all miss her, we all need her, but she isn't here and we're having to adjust. It's going to take time and patience."

"I've run out of both," Paul admitted wryly.

"So have I," she acknowledged, surprising him. "That's why I want to give my notice at the college and move in with you and the kids."

Chapter Two

"I won't hear of it," Paul said bluntly, emphatically.

Leah had fully expected an argument. Paul was proud. Being forced to accept her help, or anyone's for that matter, went against his independent nature. That he'd been forced to rely on her and his parents in the past several months was difficult enough.

"I've given the matter a good deal of thought," Leah argued.

"I appreciate the offer, but I can't allow you to do it," Paul said, smiling briefly. Others might have buckled under the obstinate look in his deep blue eyes, but over the past six months Leah had come to know her brother-in-law too well to surrender that easily.

"The boys aren't adjusting well."

"Leah, I said no," he returned firmly.

"Ryan can barely leave the house without his security blanket. We both know he has trouble going to sleep without it."

"In time he'll be willing to give it up."

"And Ronnie, dear sweet Ronnie, has taken to sucking his thumb again," she continued undaunted. "In case you haven't noticed, he's become ambidextrous about it lately, although he continues to favor the right hand."

"Both thumbs?" Paul didn't bother to disguise his shock. His eyes hardened before he repeated, "Given time the boys will adjust."

"They need stability and security."

"I'm trying," Paul said, inhaling sharply. "I'm doing everything I know how to do."

"No one's faulting you."

"I can't do everything."

"I know," Leah assured him quietly. "No one expects you to. My moving in with the four of you will only be temporary. It'll give the boys a chance to adjust to Diane's loss without all the additional upheaval they're going through now. It will help regulate Kelsey's schedule, too."

"What's wrong with her schedule?" Paul demanded.

Leah didn't want it to sound as though she were criticizing his efforts, but the six-month-old's feeding timetable was a strong element in her case.

"Kelsey should be sleeping through the nights by now."

"Then why isn't she?" Paul raked his hand through his hair, leaving deep grooves through the dark thickness.

"My guess is that you've conditioned her for a midnight feeding."

"I've done what?"

"You expect her to wake up and are so attuned to her making the slightest noise that when she does, you spring out of bed instantly."

"I had to put her crib in my room," he argued, "otherwise I didn't hear her."

"I know. I'm not faulting you, I'm just explaining that it's necessary to move her into her own room and start regulating her eating schedule a little more."

"Trust me, I'd be thrilled if Kelsey decided to sleep through the night." He rubbed a hand down his face and heaved a soul-deep sigh.

"It'd only be for a few years."

"You don't honestly expect me to agree to this, do you?"

"Just until the boys are in school full-time and Kelsey's in preschool. By then the kids won't need me as much and I'll be free to resume my teaching schedule."

Paul didn't say anything for several moments, seeming to weigh her words. Slowly he shook his head. "I appreciate the offer more than you know, but I can't let you do it. It's too much of a sacrifice."

"Diane was my sister," Leah returned softly, hoping to hide the pain that surfaced whenever she mentioned her sister's name. "Her children are the only family I have left. It wouldn't be a sacrifice—it would be something done willingly and out of love. The twins need me and so does Kelsey."

"It's not fair for you to give up your life."

"Give it up?" she repeated with a short laugh. "You make it sound like I'm offering to leap into a volcano to appease some ancient god. I'm going to take a sabbatical from teaching. That's all. Nearly every teacher takes one at some point or another in their career."

"You won't be exactly traveling, or studying though, will you?" He asked the question with a tight frown.

"No, but I'll gain a good deal more from the experience than you think. I love the children. I really want to do this."

"What about money?"

It went without saying how tight finances were currently for Paul. Diane's medical expenses had crippled him. The funeral had wiped out what savings he had, and there was the added expense of Kelsey's needs. He couldn't pay Leah, nor could he offer to reimburse her for lost wages, but she had taken all that into account.

"I have a small trust fund from my mother and grandmother. It isn't a lot of money, but it's enough to keep me in panty hose for the next couple of years."

Paul hesitated, his stubborn jaw tensing before he slowly, thoughtfully shook his head. "Your offer touches my heart, but I just can't allow you to do it."

Leah knew it would eventually come down to this. His pride was like a granite wall that needed to be scaled before he'd listen to reason.

"What about your parents?" Eric and Elizabeth Manning were her ace in the hole, and although Leah preferred not to drag them into this discussion, she knew now it was necessary. Paul's parents had retired several years before and enjoyed traveling in their motor home. But since Diane's death they'd stayed in Seattle to help Paul with the children. A few years earlier Elizabeth had been looking forward to being with Taylor, the oldest Manning daughter, when she'd been pregnant with little Eric. At that time Elizabeth had fallen and badly broken her leg. It had devastated her to miss the blessed event. Now Christy was pregnant and it looked as if, once again, Elizabeth wouldn't be there for the birth of a grandchild.

"I've been checking into having someone from the church watch the kids while Mom and Dad are away," Paul informed her stiffly.

"Strangers?" Leah prompted.

"There's nothing else I can do," he flared.

"Let me move in with you. It's the obvious answer. The kids know and love me. They'll be in their own home, with their own toys. They've had enough disruption in their young lives already. I know how hard this is for you, Paul, but you can't let your pride stand in the way."

He stood abruptly and stalked to the far side of the country-style kitchen. "It seems so unfair to you."

"But I consider it a privilege. I don't expect there'll be many other opportunities in my life to do something like this for those I love. My being here with the kids can make a difference, it can help them adjust to the loss of their mother. It isn't a sacrifice, it's an honor. Years from now I'll be able to look back and feel good about the contribution I made to shaping the children of my sister and brother-in-law, to helping them through this difficult time. I get a warm feeling just thinking about it."

Paul rubbed a hand down his face. "I don't know."

He was weakening—Leah could see it, although he was still struggling with his pride, his natural inclination to carry everything upon his own shoulders.

"It won't be for more than a few years," she reiterated.

"What about you and Bill?"

Leah smiled to herself. She'd been dating Bill Mullins for three years. They were both members of the math department at Highline Community College and shared several interests. If they were going to marry, they would have done so long before now. "What about him?" she asked.

"What does he think of this?"

"I don't know, I didn't ask him."

Paul's eyes widened with surprise.

"Bill'll understand," she assured him. Leah didn't feel it was necessary to go into the intricacies of her relationship with her fellow professor. They were friends, nothing more. They dated more for the sake of companionship than romance. Bill was divorced and had been for fifteen years. If he intended to remarry, he would have brought up the subject before now.

"How can you be so sure he won't mind? If I was dating Diane, I can tell you right now, I wouldn't take kindly to her moving in with her brother-in-law—no matter what the circumstances."

"You're not Bill."

"He'll care."

Leah ignored his concern. "There's only a couple of weeks left in the quarter, and I've already talked matters over with Dean MacKenzie. I let him know there's a strong possibility I wouldn't be returning. But he needs to know for certain soon."

Paul didn't say anything for several moments. He walked over to the teakettle, carried it back to the table and refilled their cups. "I don't have a good feeling about this."

"But you'll agree to letting me move in with you?"

He nodded slowly. "And thank God every day for a sister-in-law as unselfish as you."

"What's this?" Ryan asked, lifting a textbook from the box neatly stacked in the corner of Leah's closet.

Each of the four bedrooms was filled now. Leah chose the one across from the nursery and next to the twins' room. The master bedroom, where Paul slept, was at the far end of the long hallway.

"A book," she explained as she carefully unpacked her suitcase. She hung up one item at a time as the boys investigated several of the heavy cartons she'd brought with her. Most of her furniture had gone into storage, but she hadn't been able to part with some of her precious books. She probably wouldn't have the time or the energy to explore propositional calculus in the next couple of years; nevertheless she had hauled several boxes of books from her office with her.

"I like books," Ronnie said, taking his thumb out of his mouth long enough to tell her. He sat down on the carpet next to his brother, tucking his short legs beneath him. Ryan's tattered yellow blanket was crammed under his arm as he leafed through the text, carefully examining each page as though he understood the concepts explained. Leah didn't have the heart to tell him he was holding it upside down.

"After dinner I'll read you a story," she promised, gazing down at the two.

"Mommy used to read to us."

Unbidden, the memory of Diane together with her sons flashed into Leah's mind. It was a picture of her sister sitting on the living-room sectional with the twins serenely nestled at her side. A large book was spread open across her lap as she read aloud. The boys were half-asleep as they propped their heads against Diane's breast.

The injustice of her sister's death, the heartlessness of it, struck an unexpected blow to her midsection. Leah paused in her task, holding a silk blouse to her stomach until the disturbing image passed.

"Are you going to be our mommy now?" Ryan asked, looking up at her with curious blue eyes. Paul's eyes. Both boys had been blessed with the same shade of incredibly blue eyes that was their father's. Leah wasn't sure she'd ever seen eyes that precise color. It was the first thing she noticed whenever she met any of the Manning family.

"Mommy's in heaven, remember?" Ronnie said, poking his brother with the sharp end of his elbow.

Ryan went still for a moment and pinched his eyes closed. "Sometimes I forget what she looks like. I have to try real hard to remember."

"Here," Leah said, sitting on the end of the bed, eager to prompt the boys' memory. She reached for her purse and withdrew her wallet, snapping it open. Inside were several pictures she had of Diane, Paul and the twins. She took them out of the plastic case and handed them to the boys, who had gathered beside her.

"How come she's so fat?" Ryan asked, pointing to the first picture.

Leah smiled. "That's because you and your brother were growing inside her tummy," Leah explained, ruffling Ryan's blond hair.

"I don't remember that."

"I don't suppose you do."

"Kelsey was inside her tummy, too."

"Yes, she was," Leah said, picking Ronnie up and sitting him in her lap. "Here's a picture of you when you were born." She handed him one of the pair of them dressed in white T-shirts with protective cuffs that went over their tiny hands. A small blue ribbon was taped in each baby's fuzzy blond hair.

"Which one's me?" Ryan wanted to know.

"That one." Leah pointed to the infant on the left, although she hadn't a clue.

"What's this picture?" Ronnie asked, pulling the bottom one free from Leah's hand. She had to look herself before she could say.

"That, my young man, was Easter a few years ago." She grinned, remembering how the candy-filled baskets she'd brought the boys had been bigger than they were. Ryan and Ronnie had just started to toddle and were walking toward her when she'd snapped the picture. It was one of Leah's favorites.

She shuffled through the photographs that remained, and paused as she happened upon one of Paul and Diane together. Paul's eyes held Diane's, and it was vividly apparent how much in love they were. Leah's heart constricted. It seemed so unfair that Paul should lose Diane. Six months after her death, and he still grieved. But then, so did she.

Leah's mind often filled with questions about Diane's passing. Not medical questions, but spiritual ones. She'd never told Paul, never told anyone, about the dream.

In some ways it was what prompted her into suggesting she move in with Paul and the children. It was in the dream that Diane had asked Leah to take her place.

In retrospect Leah wished she'd thought to question Diane, argue with her, convince her to stay. Even after all these months, the vision of Diane talking to her returned to haunt Leah. Sometimes she was convinced it was a product of her own imagination. Other times, she was sure it was real.

When Diane was in the hospital and Leah was spending days at her sister's side, she would come away mentally and physically exhausted. Yet, no matter how she rationalized it, she couldn't discredit those dreamy moments when Diane had come to her. She clung to that last memory of her sister. Hung on to it. But just how much was real and how much imagined, Leah couldn't say.

At any rate Leah had kept her word. She'd moved in with Diane's family and was taking her sister's place, although she felt woefully inadequate.

Leah didn't know how she, a single woman, a college-level math professor, was going to deal with three small children on a daily basis. She didn't have all the answers, only the determination to do whatever she could to keep her promise to her sister.

There was bound to be a period of adjustment for them all, Leah realized. Paul was grateful for her help, but at the same time resentful that he needed her. It would take a while for the two of them to adjust to one another.

Leah respected Paul. He had loved her sister and was a wonderful husband and father. Although she didn't share a good deal in common with him other than their love for the children, for now that was enough.

"I'll tell you what we'll do," Leah said, tucking her arm around each child and bringing them close to her side. "We'll find some pictures of your mommy and put them up in your bedroom, so you won't forget what she looks like. How does that sound?"

"Can we put a picture of me up, too?" Ryan asked. "Just so Mommy won't forget what we look like?"

"Yes, sweetheart, we can," she whispered, and kissed the top of his head.

"Where is everyone?" Paul's voice came from the kitchen.

Leah checked her watch. She'd been so busy unpacking, the time had slipped away from her. Before she could scoot off the bed, Paul was standing in the bedroom doorway.

He wore his trench coat, a gift from Diane when he'd been hired by the Seattle daily paper. What decent journalist didn't own a trench coat, she'd teased.

"Ah-ha, here you are," Paul said, squatting down and holding out his arms to his sons. Ryan and Ronnie raced across the room to hurl themselves into their father's hold.

With a growl Paul stood, lifting both boys off the ground and hugging them close.

"Where's Kelsey?" he asked, lowering the boys back down to the carpet.

"Napping." Though now that Leah noted the time, she realized Kelsey was probably awake. She moved into the nursery, and sure enough, the little girl was ly-

ing on her back, her hands fluttering gaily at her side.
The infant grinned broadly when Leah lifted her from
the crib.

"I see you got everything moved in all right," Paul
said, following her into the nursery.

"Most everything. I'll need to make one last trip in
the morning, but that should do it."

"You've got enough room for everything?"

"Plenty," she assured him. Enough room in her
heart to nurture these precious children. Enough emotional stamina to do what needed to be done. Enough
of everything . . . she hoped.

"Dinner's almost ready," Leah said as she set Kelsey on the changing table and started to remove the infant's soggy diaper.

"I can do it," Paul said, assuming the task. "You
must be exhausted."

"I'm fine, really." But she didn't protest. Allowing
him some time alone with his daughter, Leah walked
into the kitchen.

It was difficult for Paul to accept her help, especially now that she was living in his home. Hopefully,
given time, he'd grow accustomed to her being there
and wouldn't feel the need to repay her for the sacrifice she'd made. Although she had tried several times,
she couldn't make him understand that this wasn't an
imposition.

Dinner was on the table a few minutes later. Leah
had never been much of a cook. There'd been no reason to develop the skill when the only one she was
feeding was herself. Until recently she'd survived on
frozen entrées and fast-food dinners. Diane used to
claim her unhealthy eating habits would be the end of

her. But it wasn't Leah who'd left behind an anguished family.

When they were finished, Paul cleared the table while Leah stacked the dishes in the dishwasher. Wordlessly they worked together while Ryan and Ronnie entertained their sister.

"I wish you'd let me do that," he said after a moment.

"I don't mind." There were only a handful of dishes that needed to be washed by hand, and she'd be finished with them in a few minutes.

"Perhaps *you* don't mind, but *I* do," Paul said, his words taut.

The stark, proud tone of his voice caught Leah by surprise. It wasn't going to be easy, the two of them adjusting to one another's presence.

"All right," she agreed amicably enough. She didn't know what Paul thought about her. She wondered if he had any feelings toward her one way or the other.

They'd worked together, talked occasionally, grieved with one another, wept in each other's arms—but, when it came to defining their relationship, Leah was at a loss.

She turned off the water and dried her hands. Replacing the hand towel on the thin wire rack, she glanced over at Paul, her eyes skimming his. In that one brief glance, she saw so much. His fatigue. His pain. His regret.

She was about to leave the room when Paul caught her by the arm. He dropped his hand almost immediately, his eyes finding hers. For a moment he said nothing. But his meaning was clear.

He was sorry for speaking harshly to her. Leah knew that as surely as she'd ever known anything. Something deep inside her longed to comfort him, assure him she understood. This wasn't easy on either of them.

The days passed. But the pain didn't.

They shared a common bond in their love for the children, but more than that, they'd both loved Diane. They both grieved her passing. In their own way they were each learning to survive without her.

"I didn't mean to snap at you."

"I know."

"It's just that..."

"I know, Paul, you don't have to explain. You're grateful I'm here and at the same time you wish I wasn't. You aren't going to hurt my feelings, I understand."

Leah did understand; nevertheless his words had hurt. She knew Paul hadn't meant to be insensitive, and he wasn't unfeeling. But his response to her being there, to her performing the tasks that had once been his wife's, left her feeling unwanted and lacking. Diane was the one he wanted, not Leah.

His reaction stirred awake once-forgotten inadequacies. Deeply buried resentments. Not toward Diane, but toward their mother. Diane had been the beautiful child, blond and pretty. Leah was plain, inept. While Diane had been the high school cheerleader, Leah had been the bookworm. In some ways Leah knew she'd embarrassed her mother. Diane was the golden girl. Leah common and unattractive.

It had hurt Diane more than it had Leah the way their mother had favored one sister over the other. Leah had worked hard at her studies, gained a full scholarship to the University of Washington and graduated with honors. By then their mother was gone, but Diane had been there to cheer her success. She'd always been there to boost Leah's self-confidence.

But now she was gone.

Later that same night, after the boys and Kelsey were asleep, Paul brought Leah a cup of coffee. She was sitting in front of the television mindlessly watching some situation comedy, too tired to move. She was drained. Physically and mentally exhausted.

For months Paul had carried the full load of the responsibility for the children. Leah didn't know how he'd managed for so long.

"Thanks," she said, accepting the steaming mug from his hands.

"You look beat."

"I was just wondering where the boys get their energy."

"They're a handful, aren't they?" His smile was filled with fatherly pride, and Leah found herself responding to it with one of her own.

Paul settled on the recliner across from her. He was a good-looking man. His features imperfect, rugged, but nevertheless appealing. That she would notice this now came as a surprise. In many ways it was easy to understand why he'd managed to sweep her sister off her feet.

Leah wasn't likely to forget the call Diane had made to her from Alaska nearly seven years ago. Her sister had phoned to tell her she'd married Paul Manning. Leah had been aghast. She'd never met Paul, and her sister, after an all-too-brief courtship, had decided to marry him. Leah, to say the least, was shaken.

The two had always been close. It had hurt Leah that her sister would marry a man without even talking it over with her. For a time Leah had been furious. Meeting Paul had only somewhat appeased her. It had taken time for her to adjust to her sister's marrying. The fact that Paul so obviously loved Diane had gone a long way toward soothing her pride.

"You'll get used to the boys' antics," Paul said, interrupting her thoughts.

"Does Ryan usually take his stuffed animals in the bathtub with him?"

Paul grinned. "Not generally."

"I see, so what happened tonight was in my honor?"

"Don't worry, they'll dry a little worse for wear, but they will dry...eventually."

"He can't wash his blankie?" Leah hadn't been able to persuade Ryan to let go of it for so much as an hour to run it through the washing machine. Every time she suggested it, the four-year-old clung to the stained blanket as if she had proposed burning the thing...which might not be such a bad idea, Leah thought.

Paul chuckled. "At least Ronnie's thumbs are clean."

The twin's penchant for sucking his thumb worried Leah. It was only natural that both boys sought some physical form of comfort and reassurance following their mother's death. Ryan needing his blankie and Ronnie his thumb were probably classic textbook cases. But it'd been six months, and neither boy showed any sign of their need lessening.

"We're going to be all right," Paul said, closing his eyes and leaning his head against the back of his recliner. "There were times I wondered, but now for the first time since the funeral, I believe it."

"Me, too."

Paul sighed, straightened and then took a sip from his coffee. After a moment he stared blankly toward the television screen.

"I miss Diane most right about now each night," he said, his voice low and infinitely sad. "We used to sit and talk after the boys were asleep. She'd put her head on my shoulder and tell me about her day, and I'd talk to her about mine. I've tried a hundred times to remember the things we said that seemed so important, to resurrect the good feelings I had holding her in my arms, but you know, I can't remember a single word of our conversation. Not one word."

"It was just having her there listening that was important."

Paul nodded. "I suppose you're right." But he didn't sound convinced. His wife was far more than a sounding board.

They didn't often talk about Diane. She guessed it was natural for them, being thrust together like this—her first night in his home—for them to discuss the one who had unintentionally brought them to this point.

"You know what I miss about her the most?" Leah asked.

"No."

"Shopping at the mall."

Paul chuckled. "I should have guessed as much. I've never been able to understand what it is about walking from store to store that intrigues you women."

"Diane had an incredible knack for finding a bargain."

"You mean she had an incredible knack for spending money, don't you?"

Leah scooted her legs under her and smiled. "It wasn't so much the shopping expeditions, but the times we spent laughing when we tried on clothes and ordered cheesecake for lunch and then, feeling guilty, salad for dessert."

Leah's stomach knotted at the pain that came into Paul's eyes. The pain she heard in his voice. A look that was reflected in her own. A grief that echoed in her own words.

It was supposed to get easier, but she'd never missed her sister more than she did at that moment. Missing Diane hurt so terribly. For months Leah had kept the ache of loneliness to herself, not daring to discuss it with Paul, knowing he was dealing with his own pain in his own way. It felt good to release some of that anguish now.

"We're going to be all right," Paul said after a moment.

"Yes, I think we will," she returned.

In their own way they were both coping. How well, remained to be seen.

For a long while Paul said nothing.

Neither did Leah.

It was as though Paul had crawled deep inside himself, where the memories were buried, where he often adjourned in an effort to find solace. Leah understood. She'd spent a good deal of time searching out her own peace.

Unfortunately any serenity she'd found had never seemed to last long. All too soon reality would rear its ugly face, and she'd be pushed back into the present. The lonely, solitary present.

They sat for several minutes, neither speaking, neither feeling the need.

Visibly Paul relaxed. He finished his coffee, then set aside his mug and, leaning his head against the back of the recliner, closed his eyes.

Leah finished the last of her coffee, knowing that she could either go to bed immediately or fall asleep right there on the sectional.

The day had been more tiring than she'd realized. Her bones ached from the exertion of moving. From the mental fatigue of dealing with the unending demands of two preschoolers and an infant.

"Good night, Paul," she said, unfolding her legs and awkwardly standing. Her feet didn't seem to want to cooperate.

"'Night, Diane."

Chapter Three

Diane.

Paul's eyes shot open. For a moment it had almost seemed as if Diane had been in the living room with him. Almost as if he were chuckling over Ryan's mischievous nature with his much-loved wife. Only that was impossible. It had all seemed so natural. So right. Then, a slip of the tongue that nearly crippled him with grief.

For an agonizing moment he was at a loss for words. It had been a natural mistake, he supposed. Under the circumstances an understandable mistake. Certainly a forgivable one.

"I'm sorry," he said, looking to Leah, hoping he hadn't offended her.

"No problem." She reassured him with a quiet smile and headed toward the bedroom.

Paul reached for his coffee and noticed his hand was shaking as he raised the mug to his lips.

Diane.

Sometimes he wondered if the ache of her loss would ever ease. She'd been gone half a year, yet his grief was as powerful now as it had been that fateful night when Dr. Charman had called him to the hospital.

In the time since her funeral, Paul had experienced a full scale of emotions. Unleashed fear. Burning anger. And occasionally a lopsided acceptance. Just when he felt as though he'd moved beyond the corridor of pain, something more would happen, and he'd be forced to deal with each series of emotions all over again as if facing them for the first time.

He was grateful to Leah, although he hadn't been nearly as gracious as he should have been when she'd offered to move in with him and the children. He liked Diane's older sister. She was a generous woman, and he'd always be grateful to her for the commitment she'd made to helping him with the children. Frankly Paul didn't know what he would have done thus far without her. He recalled the first time he met her, and how surprised he'd been by Diane's sister. He had expected another Diane. Someone so full of life and laughter that her smile rivaled the brilliance of the sun. Erroneously he'd imagined she'd be blond and pretty, the way his young wife was.

Leah was neither.

She wasn't unattractive—he wouldn't describe her as plain. As a writer he should be able to find some way to adequately depict her. Yet each word that came into his mind, he ended up discarding. At one time he'd thought of her as mousy and nondescript.

He'd since changed his mind.

There was a subdued radiance to her, a joy and cheerfulness that broke through her natural restraints every now and again when he wasn't expecting to see it. It never failed to charm him.

She'd always been Ryan and Ronnie's favorite relative. It had been Leah who'd comforted them when they'd learned about their mother. It had been Leah who'd encouraged them when Paul had had no reassurances to give. It had been Leah who'd played and cheered them when he didn't know if he'd ever find the strength to laugh again.

That afternoon had been a good example of the woman he knew Leah to be. He'd returned from the newspaper office to find her in her bedroom with the boys gathered around her. When he'd walked into the room, she'd looked up and smiled...and for a moment, just a tiny, infinitesimal moment, Paul had felt whole again.

Over coffee that evening he'd experienced that same sense of wholeness, as though the crushing weight he'd been carrying since Diane's death had been eased. Not by much, but enough for some of the numbness to leave his heart.

He'd always be grateful to Leah. He owed her a debt several lifetimes couldn't repay. Although he didn't want to own up to it, he was pleased she was there with him and the children. He'd promised himself he wouldn't take advantage of her generosity. He'd make sure she had time to herself, time to get away, socialize, do whatever it was she needed to do to keep her sanity over the next couple of years.

It was the least he could do. She, after all, was essential to him maintaining his.

A month passed, the easiest weeks for Paul since Diane's death. Each day he felt less embittered, less confused, less weakened. He'd even started thinking about working on his novel again. The anticipation cheered him.

The transition from college professor to housekeeper-mother hadn't been easy for Leah, Paul realized, but she was managing exceptionally well. He was proud of the progress she'd made. Her efforts around the house had made a tremendous difference. She'd even taken on some of the yard work and with Ryan and Ronnie's help was planting a garden.

All three of the children were thriving under her attention and care. Paul couldn't believe the difference in his sons. Ryan forgot to drag his blankie with him every so often now. He was watching cartoons without it one afternoon that week when Paul had arrived home from work. Ronnie was at his brother's side, and for the first time in recent memory, his son's thumb wasn't in his mouth.

Paul had praised Leah, but she'd quickly brushed off his compliments, claiming the changes in the boys' behavior weren't due solely to her, but to the number of other factors. Although the boys were more secure in their own home now that she was there to take care of them, attending the preschool with their neighborhood friends had helped, too. And the summer sunshine, she contended, that also contributed.

Although Paul didn't fully agree with her, he had let it pass. Leah wasn't comfortable with his appreciation.

He used to think of her as quiet and unassuming. But in the past few weeks he realized he was only partially right. She was sensitive and loving, and her gentleness was a soothing balm that was healing them all.

The phone on his desk rang, and Paul automatically reached for it.

"Hi ya, there, big brother," the deep male voice greeted.

"Rich, hello." Paul hadn't heard from his brothers much lately. Mostly it was his fault. He'd spurned their efforts to draw him out after Diane's death. Both Rich and Jason were on a softball team and they'd wanted him to join them for a summer league. Paul had nearly laughed out loud. There wasn't time for sports in his life. He was struggling to make it from one day into the next. At the time the thought of playing softball had seemed ludicrous considering the loss he'd endured. In hindsight Paul realized Rich and Jason were only trying to help, but he hadn't been ready.

"Rich, it's good to hear from you," Paul said, meaning it.

"You might have called me," the youngest Manning brother chastised.

"True enough."

"You're fortunate I'm willing to overlook your impropriety, but I'll let you make it up to me."

"I knew you would."

"Actually I'm calling to ask a small favor." Some of the teasing laughter drained from Rich's voice.

"Oh?" Paul didn't have a lot to give these days.

"One of the guys on the softball team, Harry Duncan . . . you remember Harry, don't you? The auto mechanic from the garage off Seventy-sixth?"

"Yeah." Paul vaguely remembered meeting the man. "What about him?"

"He's going to have to miss the next couple of softball games. Jason and I were talking it over and we thought . . . since Leah's taking care of the kids now, that you might be able to get away for a couple of Saturday mornings. Listen, if you need to bring the twins, that'd work out. Jamie always comes to the games and I'm sure she wouldn't mind looking after them."

Despite himself Paul chuckled.

"What's so funny?"

"I'd thought you would have learned by now, little brother."

"Learned what?"

"Not to volunteer your wife for something until you've checked with her first."

"Oh . . . right, I suppose I shouldn't, but the team's desperate. Harry's a good shortstop, but not nearly as good as you."

"Do you figure buttering me up's going to help?"

"I was hoping," Rich admitted honestly. "Do you think you could do it?"

"Let me get back to you."

"When?"

"This evening," Paul promised.

He was tempted. Damn tempted. Leah wouldn't mind—he knew that without asking. She'd be the first one to encourage him to do it.

Maybe he would, Paul decided . . . just maybe he would.

* * *

"You're sure you don't mind?" Paul asked for the
third time the following Saturday morning. He
couldn't help feeling a tad guilty about abandoning
Leah with the kids while he went off with his brothers.

"Paul," she chided, smiling up at him. "Go, before
I push you out the door. I've got plans myself."

"Planting a garden sounds more like work to me."
A variety of egg cartons cluttered the kitchen counter-
top. Leah and the boys had been enthusiastically
working on the project for weeks.

Somehow they'd gotten him involved. Two week-
ends before, he'd found himself spading up a section
of the yard for them to use. When he'd finished, Leah
and the boys had dumped topsoil and fertilizer on the
area, working feverishly to spread it evenly over the
rough surface.

Then the eggshells started turning up. One afternoon recently he'd found the three of them filling
halves of eggshells with potting soil and then inserting
a single seed. Now the shells were filled with sprouting
zucchini, cucumber, radish and lettuce plants.

The young plants, Leah declared that morning, were
now healthy and strong enough to be transplanted
outside.

Paul's sons had been delighted with the idea. More
than once he'd found the two of them peering over the
kitchen counter, as if they were hoping to catch the
seeds instantaneously hatching into full-grown plants.

"I could bring Kelsey with me," he offered.

"She'll go down late for her nap and be crabby. You
don't need that." She carried the boys' empty cereal
bowls to the sink. "Now, hurry or you'll be late."

Paul downed the last of his coffee. As she strolled past, Leah grabbed the bill of his baseball cap and pushed it downward until it bounced against the tip of his nose. "Have fun, Mickey Mantle," she teased.

Paul laughed, straightened the cap and reached for his mitt. It wasn't until he was outside starting up his car that he realized it had been a good long while since he'd felt so lighthearted.

Paul couldn't remember a morning he'd enjoyed more since Diane's death. His softball skills were a bit rusty, but he'd made a diving catch and caught a ground ball that had turned the tide of the game. His brothers had slapped him across the back and run off the field with him. One would have thought he was playing in the World Series for all the praise that was heaped on him.

Damn, but it felt good to get out like this. It didn't hurt to laugh. He didn't feel guilty to be having fun. It felt right to be with his brothers. A good kind of right.

Jamie, Rich's wife, had packed a picnic lunch for after the game and invited Paul to join her and Rich, but he declined, anxious to return home.

Jason eagerly accepted their invitation, and Paul was glad to see it—his two brothers together—his sister-in-law so kind and pleasant. Although Jamie had been a part of the family for the better part of two years, it never ceased to surprise him that his playboy brother had married her. Of the three of them, Rich had been blessed with the best looks. His tall, compelling presence had garnered him attention from the opposite sex since he was in junior high. He could have had his pick of women.

Yet he'd married Jamie. Paul liked her. In fact, he liked his sister-in-law quite a bit; he'd been surprised to find her so unpretentious, even just a little ordinary. In many ways she was a lot like Leah.

A sigh came to him as he thought of Diane's sister. Leah, ordinary? She was about as average as the Hope Diamond. A sensation of grateful tenderness took hold of him as he mulled over the changes Leah had brought into his life in the past month. The changes she'd made in his children's lives. Her gentle warmth had largely gone unnoticed until she'd moved in with him. Her optimism. Her smile, too.

There was something special to her smile that defied description. Just the way it gently lifted the corners of her mouth and then worked its way into her eyes. He'd always thought Leah's hazel eyes were plain. It amazed him how blind he could have been to their versatility. If she wore green, her eyes were green. If she had on something blue, her eyes showed hints of blue. If she wore something dark, then the brown highlights revealed themselves.

Her eyes were a lot like Leah herself, Paul decided. Adaptable. Multifaceted.

He'd come to know Leah in the past month. Really *know* her. Appreciate her and her quiet ways. He'd tried to analyze what had happened to him since her arrival in his home, but he couldn't make sense of it. When she had first arrived, he'd been consumed with his grief, holding on to it with both hands. In many ways he'd been afraid to let go. What was there left for him if he didn't have his grief? Emptiness? A looming black hole that threatened to swallow him.

After the first week that Leah had moved in, he noticed there'd be stretches of time without the harsh emotional pain choking him. He'd feel almost free. Then something would happen to remind him of how lonely he was without Diane, and the pain would return full force.

Pain.

No pain.

Pain again, but not as black or as deep as before. Still there, but just enough for him to be conscious of it.

Then gone again.

Paul found it curious that Diane's sister could have brought about so dramatic a change in him. More curious still that someone who for the most part was a stranger to him, would ease the misery of his soul.

Paul pulled into the driveway of his home, eager to see Leah and the children. Eager to view their progress in the garden. He stuck his softball mitt in the hall closet and grabbed a cold soda from the refrigerator. He'd pulled back the tab and was tasting his first swallow when he happened to look out the sliding glass door.

Paul froze.

The aluminum pop can was poised in front of his mouth as he viewed the scene in front of him. Kelsey was sitting in her walker, small arms stretched upward attempting to catch a butterfly. The boys were digging with hand shovels, their young faces intent on the task with Leah looking on, laughing at something one of them said.

The sound of her laughter drifted toward him, and Paul swore he had never heard anything more beautiful. Not music. Not joy. Not anything.

She was wearing faded jeans and a short-sleeved blouse. She'd left the bottom two buttons of the shirt unfastened and had knotted the tails at her waist. Her hair had caught in the wind, and the sunshine cast a golden iridescent glow through the fine strands.

Paul's heart constricted, not with pain, as he was accustomed to feeling. He almost wished it was pain. He knew how to deal with that, how to react. But it wasn't pain he felt now.

It was desire.

A desire so gut wrenching, so deep, it took his breath away. It wasn't sexual need. He didn't want to ravish Leah's body, or seek physical satisfaction. He'd never thought of her in those terms, never considered what it would be like to make love to anyone other than his wife, who was seven months in the grave. What Paul felt, what he was feeling, was something totally beyond his realm of experience. Almost spiritual in nature, if he were to try to put words to it.

Strange as it seemed, he experienced the overwhelming urge to sit down and weep. Sobs burned for release, tightening his chest, thickening his throat. With some effort he was able to hold them at bay.

Hours later Paul wasn't sure what it was about the scene that had struck him so hard. The simplicity of it, he supposed, perhaps the gentle beauty of those precious moments.

The sky had been blue and the sunshine beaming down like God's smile on those he cherished most. It came to Paul then. Clearly. Keenly. For a moment he was amazed at how obtuse he'd been. What had affected him so strongly was...life. How glorious life can be. How beautiful. How precious.

For months he'd been in the dark, voluntarily lingering in the stark coolness of the shadows. The sudden contrast between the light and the dark had seemed so profound.

When Leah had first arrived, Paul had been dying. He'd wanted to die with Diane. A month had passed and he'd discovered, much to his surprise, he wanted to live.

Leah's shoulders ached. She'd worked most of the morning in the garden with the boys. Unaccustomed as she was to physical exercise, it was little wonder that her muscles were rebelling. Following lunch, she'd taken a long, hot shower and changed clothes. The boys were tired; they'd gone down for their nap with nary a complaint.

The house was quiet. Paul was working in his den, the boys and Kelsey were sound asleep, and Leah reached for her library book. Reading for pleasure was something she'd missed over the past several years. But no more than five minutes into the first chapter, her eyes kept drifting shut.

She woke shortly after three, surprised to find a blanket over her shoulders.

"Good afternoon, Sleeping Beauty," Paul teased when she opened her eyes.

Sitting up, disorientated, Leah glanced about her. The last thing she remembered was setting aside the library book and resting her eyes. Only for a moment, she'd promised herself. She'd given up napping when she started first grade.

"The garden looks great."

Leah's smile was filled with pride. "Thank you. The boys and I worked hard."

"I can tell. They're awake, by the way."

"And hungry, too, no doubt." She automatically tossed aside the blanket, ready to meet the demands of her two nephews.

"Don't worry about it. We walked down to the store for ice-cream bars. Kelsey went along for the ride, too."

"Is Leah awake yet?" Ryan asked eagerly as he vaulted into the living room. He beamed her a wide grin when he saw that she was. "Did you tell her about the surprise?" he asked, looking up at his father.

"Not yet."

"What surprise?"

"It's nothing big," Paul explained. "We brought you back an ice-cream bar, too. I hope you like double fudge."

"I love it. Thank you, Paul." She smiled up at him and, closing her eyes, stretched her arms high above her head and yawned once more.

When she'd finished, he was still watching her, but he was wearing a frown, something she hadn't seen him do of late, then he turned abruptly and moved into the kitchen.

Leah followed and Ronnie, struggling with his brother, opened the freezer and brought out the ice-cream bar they'd bought for her. She sat at the table and opened the small box. It had melted a little on the walk home.

Paul pulled out the chair, twisted it around and straddled it. "When was the last time you talked to Bill?" he asked unexpectedly.

"Bill?" she repeated, surprised Paul would ask about him. "I don't know, I haven't thought about it."

"Don't you think it's time the two of you went out?"

"No." Contrary to what Paul seemed to think, her relationship with her fellow professor wasn't on a timetable. It must seem strange to someone like her brother-in-law, who felt so deeply about people and things.

"Shouldn't you call him, then?"

"Not really."

Paul frowned. "Don't you care?"

She shrugged. "I suppose."

"Then call." He moved off the chair and took the telephone receiver off the hook and handed it to her.

"Paul?"

"I insist."

"All right, all right," she said with a resigned sigh. She didn't know why it was so all-fired important all of a sudden for her to contact Bill, but in an effort to appease Paul, she'd do it.

As it turned out, Bill sounded pleased to hear from her and suggested they go out to the movies that evening. When she mentioned it to Paul, he seemed relieved. Pleased.

She found his response puzzling, but shrugged it off.

"You look nice," he told her when she had changed clothes several hours later. He was reading the evening paper, the very one that employed him, when Bill arrived.

Bill, in his late forties, had never been Leah's heart-throb. She sincerely doubted that he'd ever been any woman's heartthrob. He wore a gray cardigan sweater, the same one he'd worn every time they'd gone out, other than to faculty dinners, for the past three years.

Leah introduced the two men. Bill stepped forward and shook Paul's hand. Her date was a bit nervous, Leah noted, which surprised her.

The boys each wanted a hug, which she willingly gave them. They started to follow her to the door, but Paul distracted their attention and she was able to leave without them asking Bill a lot of questions, something they would have loved to have done.

The evening was clear and bright. Generally June's weather was mild in the Pacific Northwest. This June was no exception.

"It's good to see you again," Bill said as he helped her into the car. He'd always been a gentleman, and it was the small touches, the old-fashioned manners, that made him so endearing. No one was going to define sex appeal by using Bill Mullins as an example, but, for the most part, he was considerate and kind.

"It's good to see you."

He walked around the front of the car and joined her in the front seat. "The college seems empty without you."

"Summer quarter's pretty slow anyway," she said, brushing off his words.

"True, but I always knew you'd be back come fall. It's not going to be the same without you, Leah."

He surprised her by blushing. This was probably the most romantic thing he'd said to her in the three years they'd been dating.

Bill seemed flustered as he inserted the key in the ignition and started the engine. Leah reached for the seat belt, locking it in place. Bill twisted around to check behind him before backing out of the driveway, and as he did, a movement in the front of the house caught Leah's attention.

The twins were at the front window, their grubby hands pressing against the pane, watching her with round blue eyes. She smiled and waved.

Ryan waved back, but Ronnie didn't.

Instead his thumb went into his mouth.

Leah frowned. Ronnie seldom sucked his thumb these days. He was working hard at breaking the habit.

Her eyes were still on the front window when Paul appeared, standing behind his sons. His gaze connected with hers, and something strong and undefinable passed between them. The sheer depth, the sheer power of that brief moment, left Leah breathless.

Leah's pulse burst into a rapid-fire speed.

Could it be regret she read in Paul's eyes? That made no sense. The moment was all too brief to be sure. Much too short to be telling.

What it was, if it was anything at all, Leah couldn't say. By then Bill had driven past the house and the moment was lost.

Leah dropped her gaze to her hands, surprised to find them clenched tightly in her lap. Could it be that Paul hadn't wanted her to go out with Bill? That was ridiculous. He'd practically arranged the date himself.

Although it was shortly after ten when Bill drove her home, the house was dark and quiet.

"Would you like to come inside for coffee?" she invited.

"Not tonight, thanks."

Leah hated to admit how grateful she was that he opted not to. They hadn't had much time to talk. The movie had dominated the evening, giving them little time alone. Although Bill hadn't said much, Leah knew he was uneasy with her living situation. He didn't ask her any direct questions about Paul, but he had hinted that he feared something romantic might be developing between Leah and her brother-in-law.

She'd let his insinuations go unanswered. To deny anything would have invited argument. If it hadn't been so ludicrous a suggestion, Leah might have laughed.

Paul had loved Diane. Her sister had been beautiful and vivacious. Leah was neither. Diane had been witty and charming. Leah lacked both skills. After loving Diane, there was little chance Paul would ever feel anything more than gratitude for Leah.

"Could I see you again?" Bill asked her, sounding a bit flustered.

"Of course."

"Next week . . . sometime?"

"That would be fine."

Bill grinned, looking pleased. "I'll give you a call, then . . . say Monday evening?"

"I'll be here."

He climbed out of the car and walked around to her side and opened the door. He offered her his hand, which she accepted, and then he escorted her to the front door. Once again he seemed a little ill at ease. They'd only kissed occasionally. Light kisses. Nothing urgent and certainly nothing close to passionate.

Bill wrapped his arms around her waist and gently pulled her closer. He gave her the opportunity to object and, when she didn't, he brought his mouth down to hers. It was by far the most ardent kiss they'd ever exchanged. But Leah had the feeling he was testing her with it, attempting another means of discovering if there was anything romantic going on between her and Paul.

He broke off the kiss abruptly and stared down at her, reading her expression.

"Good night, Bill," she said, breaking free of his crushing embrace. "I'll talk to you next week."

Bill released her immediately. "Right," he said, sounding breathless and uncertain. "I'll phone you Monday."

Leah let herself into the house and, leaning against the door, she sighed. Not with pleasure, but with relief. The movie had been entertaining, and Paul was right—it probably did her good to get away for a few hours. But she hadn't enjoyed herself the way she'd thought she would.

Bill had seemed—she hated to say it—dull. If he wasn't hinting at a romance between her and Paul, he was making her sound like a martyr for moving in with Paul and the children. Nothing short of Joan of Arc. It had made Leah uncomfortable.

A sliver of light sneaked out from the crack under the door in Paul's den, and Leah was half-tempted to politely tell him she was home.

Before she could make up her mind if she should, Paul came out.

"I thought I heard you," he said, greeting her with a warm smile. He smiled more often these days, and she marveled at how it involved his whole face, though it never seemed to cut through the pain that marked his eyes.

"I'm home," she announced, feeling slightly nervous and not knowing why.

"How was it?"

"Fine. We went to a movie."

Paul nodded and buried his hands in his pants pockets, striking a relaxed pose. "I'm glad you got away for a few hours."

"You're just feeling guilty about playing softball with your brothers this morning," she teased. "Would you like some coffee?"

"Yeah," he said, following her into the kitchen, "I would."

Leah filled two mugs with water and stuck them in the microwave. Neither one of them would be interested in drinking a full pot.

"You should have invited Bill in."

"I did," she said, her back to him as she set the dials on the microwave.

"Why didn't he come inside?"

Leah shrugged. "I don't know."

"Because of me?"

"He didn't say." She turned around and folded her arms, waiting for the timer to ding so she could add instant coffee to the hot water.

"You'll be seeing him again soon, won't you?"

Chapter Four

"Yes," Leah confirmed, frowning. It dented her pride that Paul seemed so eager to have her out of his home. "Bill and I will be dating again soon."

Paul nodded. "Good idea."

"Good idea?" Leah laughed as she finished stirring the instant coffee into the hot water. "Why's that?" she asked as she handed Paul a mug.

He led the way to the kitchen table and pulled out the rail-back chair. "It eases my mind."

His answer made no sense to Leah. He must have read the question in her eyes, because he elaborated.

"There's nothing I can do to reimburse you for everything you've done, Leah. I can't afford to pay you."

"Paul..."

"I don't own anything valuable enough to give you."

"But, Paul..."

"It seems like such a little thing to make certain you get out every once in a while. I want to be sure you have ample opportunity to do so."

Paul lowered his gaze to his coffee, his hands enclosing the mug in a tight grip.

"It hasn't been so bad, you know?" Leah wished she knew of some way to reassure him. Yes, it had taken her a few weeks to work out a schedule for her and the children, and yes, she'd been exhausted by the end of most days. But she wasn't a noble priestess, as Paul and Bill were making her out to be. Mothering the children was something she wanted to do. Already she was reaping rewards beyond anything she'd dreamed.

"I want you to have fun," Paul said emphatically.

"Oh, Paul," she breathed. "Don't you think I am? Kelsey, the boys and I had a marvelous time today planting our garden. I'll have those memories all my life. This morning with the children was the most precious part of my day, not my time with Bill."

"You should slow down, then," he continued gruffly. "There isn't any need to keep the house and yard spotless. I feel guilty enough as it is without you working all hours of the day and night."

If Leah had ever heard a gross exaggeration, this was it. Her housekeeping skills were best described as adequate. Her interest in planting a garden had come as the result of a project the boys had brought home from preschool—a small plant growing from inside a Dixie cup. She had worked hard on the garden, but it had been a labor of love, and not because she felt a burning need to make the yard into a showplace.

She couldn't, she wouldn't slow down, though. It was partly her sense of duty, partly her need to keep busy. This was her first experience outside of a classroom since she was five years old. There was a whole lot out there for her to explore, and she was eager to do so. She was finding her footing. *Learning the ropes* was the phrase that came to mind.

"I'm enjoying myself."

Paul looked as though he wasn't sure he should believe her.

"I am, honest." She reached forward and placed her hand over his forearm in an effort to convince him. The action had been instinctive, but the instant her hand closed over Paul's arm, Leah realized it was a mistake. She wasn't sure why, except that her heart leapt. One strong, fast burst of power surged through her.

Even hours later as she lay awake in bed, her mind refused to let go of that moment when they'd touched, as brief as it had been. She'd lifted her hand almost immediately, and the conversation had continued, but something had changed.

Only Leah didn't know what it was.

She wasn't good when it came to relationships. She'd never been good with them. She recognized love. Love was easy. Her feelings toward Kelsey and the twins were as strong as any mother's. Diane may have given birth to the children, but Leah was the one taking her sister's place and her protectiveness toward those three little ones was fierce.

In some ways she supposed she loved Paul, too, Leah mused. But on a much less definable level.

They'd bonded. That was the only logical explanation she could give for what happened to her when she'd touched his arm. They'd been through so much together. Shared so many things. The trauma of Diane's death. Her funeral. And now the raising of the children. Naturally there was a bond between them. It would be implausible for there not to be, especially with them living together the way they did.

This bonding phenomenon would explain the physical response she experienced when she'd touched him. It wasn't a sexual response. Or was it? Leah didn't know. If she'd had more experience with relationships, she might be able to better define it.

Bill had touched her that night, too. His kiss had been probing and urgent. She hadn't liked it, had wanted to rub her hand over her lips and erase it when he'd finished.

How different it was with Paul. Her senses had leapt to life, and she'd been intimately aware of him. Their gazes had met, and his eyes had relentlessly stared into hers.

Bill had kissed her, and she hadn't felt so much as a fraction of the sensation she had when she'd brushed her fingers over Paul's skin. But it was Bill she was dating. Bill she would be spending time with. Bill who'd asked her out.

Now that she had time to think about it, Leah realized she would prefer it if Bill didn't phone her next week. His insinuations about her and Paul had insulted her, but she hadn't known how irate she was until it was too late to say anything.

Leah felt trapped.

Bill seemed eager to continue their relationship while she felt utterly content without him, satisfied with putting everything between them on hold. True, she'd been the one to contact him, but only because Paul had insisted.

That opportunity to put Bill on the back shelf of her life had been taken away from her, however. Paul seemed to find it a matter of pride that she continue dating her fellow professor. As though this was the one thing he could do to ease her heavy load. He made the rigors of taking care of the children sound as if she were part of a chain gang. Nothing she could say was able to convince him she was pleased with the status quo.

Her inability to put her feelings into words frustrated Leah. For the first time since Diane's death, she felt as though the black cloud of her anguish had lifted. The children had greatly boosted her spirits, returning to her the precious gift of laughter. It felt incredibly good to wrap her arms around the three little ones who had indelibly touched her life, and let go of her grief. She discovered she couldn't hold on to the emotional pain of losing her sister and the children both at the same time.

Leah smiled to herself in the dark. She hadn't thought of it in those terms before, but it was true. The children's reaction to their mother's death was buried deep in their psyches. Evidence of this revealed itself in Ryan needing his blankie and Ronnie his thumb. But on the surface they were the same little boys they'd always been. Giddy, mischievous, openly curious—they were her heart's delight.

Leah couldn't be around the children and continue the melancholy patterns that grief had brought into her life. *She* was the one who had benefited by coming to live with them. Now if she could only make Paul understand and accept that.

* * *

As he'd promised, Bill phoned Leah Monday evening, right after she'd finished clearing the dishes off the dinner table. Paul answered the phone and, without a word, handed her the receiver. Although he moved out of the kitchen to grant her some privacy, she couldn't shake the feeling that wherever he was, he was able to listen in on her conversation.

"Hello, Leah."

"Bill."

"How are you?"

"Fine, thanks, and you?"

"Good. Real good."

She wondered if their conversation could get any more banal. "I'm pleased to hear it."

"Will you be free Saturday evening?"

"Ah...yes, I shouldn't have any problem getting away." Paul would make sure of that.

"Great. I was thinking about a poetry reading in Blaine. I know it's a bit of a ways to drive, and we probably won't get back until late, but I think the effort will be worth it."

"That sounds great." It sounded utterly boring, but Leah didn't feel that she had any other option. If she made an excuse to Bill, he'd be convinced there really was something between her and Paul. And Paul, bless his heart, seemed to find it vitally important that she date Bill.

Leah didn't have a lot of friends. Her best friend had always been her sister, and her only other really good friend, Linda Potter, was traveling in Europe this summer. Getting out occasionally with Linda might have eased Paul's concern, but with her only other friend away, Leah was stuck with Bill.

"Wonderful. I'll pick you up around six, then," Bill said, sounding pleased.

They spoke a few minutes more, the same insipid discourse that had marked the first minutes of the call. Leah hung up the receiver, wondering what it was about Bill that had ever interested her. Instinctively she realized it wasn't Bill who'd changed, but herself.

No sooner had she finished on the phone than Paul entered the kitchen, his eyes searching out hers.

"That was Bill," she explained unnecessarily.

"I gathered as much," he said evenly, revealing no emotion.

"We're going out again this Saturday evening." She didn't have the courage to tell him it was to a poetry reading for fear Paul might laugh, and then she would, too. And laughter between them would be so intimate.

The doorbell chimed just then, and Paul, looking as though he meant to say something more, left to answer it. Leah didn't know if she should be grateful or not for the interruption.

She was placing the last of the dinner dishes in the dishwasher when Elizabeth Manning walked into the kitchen, smiling affectionately when she saw Leah.

"Hello, Leah."

"Hello," she greeted Paul's mother warmly, drying her hands on a kitchen towel. Before Diane's passing, the elder Mannings had been mere acquaintances, but over the past several months Leah had come to love and appreciate Paul's parents. "When did you get back?"

"This morning."

At the sound of their grandmother's voice, the twins raced out of the back bedroom and hurled themselves at Elizabeth's legs, holding on and squeezing tightly as they cried out their excitement.

Elizabeth laughed and reached down to hug her two grandsons.

Leah smiled herself. The boys had missed their grandparents. After she'd come to live with Paul, the older Mannings had taken a two week sojourn down the Oregon coast in their motor home.

"There's coffee made," Leah said, bringing down four cups while Elizabeth brought out two giant seashells she'd brought back for the twins. Ryan and Ronnie were delighted with their gifts and then dragged their grandmother down the hallway to show her the picture of their mother that Leah had put up in their bedroom.

When she'd finished pouring the coffee, Leah carried the tray into the living room, where Paul was sitting with his father. Paul glanced up and smiled his appreciation.

Elizabeth returned with the twins and the four sat down. Elizabeth and Eric were on the sectional. Paul was in his recliner and Leah across from him. Kelsey was scooting around in her walker, and after a moment Elizabeth reached for her granddaughter, who struggled momentarily, then settled down in Elizabeth's lap to investigate her necklace and then taste it.

"It's good to be home," Eric was saying to Paul. "I suppose we should have phoned first, but we were eager to see how everything was working out with you."

"We're fine, Dad." Paul's gaze drifted to Leah.

It had been going well, better than either Paul or Leah had expected it would. There'd been some adjusting on both their parts, but it had been minimal. The children were thriving. For a long moment Leah and Paul simply stared at one another.

It was Leah who realized she needed to say something to break the silence. "Everything is working out just great," she confirmed, then cleared her throat. She was grateful when Ryan scooted onto her lap. Not wanting to be outdone by his brother, Ronnie joined him. Leah had to peek out from behind the boys' backs. "The twins and I went down earlier this week and registered for kindergarten classes."

"We went to the big kids' school," Ryan explained eagerly.

"Since the boys have summer birthdays, I was a little concerned about them being ready for kindergarten," Leah explained.

"Leah had them tested, and it looks like everything's a go," Paul said, sounding pleased.

"Although I did request the morning session," Leah added. "The boys still need their naps."

"We do not," Ronnie righteously denied. "I'm almost five." He held up his hand and proudly splayed his fingers. Ryan quickly pantomimed his brother.

"I remember when Paul and his brothers were that age," Elizabeth said, smiling broadly. "Your daddy felt the same way. 'Five-year-olds are too old to nap,' he insisted, but I put him down every afternoon simply because I needed the peace and quiet myself."

"I'm thirty-six years old," Paul said, looking to Leah, "and my mother still tells tales about me."

"I always will," Elizabeth chided gently. "It doesn't matter how old you are, you'll always be my little boy."

Paul's parents left an hour later, after relaying a few of their adventures while camping along the Oregon coast. The visit was a good one.

Leah envied Paul his family. He'd always been close to his siblings and his parents. Leah and Diane only had each other. Their mother had several personality problems, and their father had abandoned the family when the girls were barely old enough to remember him. Leah's own grandparents lived on the other side of the country, and she could only recall visiting them one time. They'd both died when she was in her teens.

Diane had loved Paul's family, too. She had never complained about problems with her in-laws, and made it a point to give Paul ample opportunity to do things with Jason and Rich, his two younger brothers.

Leah wasn't well acquainted with Paul's siblings, but she knew they'd all pulled together to help Paul after Diane's passing, offering to do whatever they could to help him cope. Paul's pride had stood in the way, and he'd systematically rebuffed their efforts. He grudgingly accepted hers, Leah realized, but only because he'd had no other option.

Times were better now. They were all learning to adapt. The changes that were taking place were positive ones and for that, Leah was grateful.

Paul didn't know what was wrong with him. He'd been in a foul mood most of the evening. Impatient and restless. Leah's date had arrived shortly after dinner, and Paul had barely been able to look at the man.

Ryan had wanted ice cream sometime later, and for no reason at all, Paul found himself saying no. The boys had looked surprised to have him snap at them and quickly retreated to their bedroom.

Feeling guilty, Paul had followed them, apologized and then together the three had dished out huge bowls of ice cream. The boys had insisted upon putting on their own topping and had smeared chocolate syrup all over the counter. Paul had been sure to clean up the mess.

He didn't want Leah coming home from her night on the town to find the kitchen a disaster.

The day had been a good one, too, which further confused Paul. If he'd had to deal with one frustrating event after another, he might be entitled to a foul mood. But he hadn't.

The morning had started out great when he'd played softball with his brothers. He had forgotten how much he enjoyed sports, and was disappointed Harry Duncan would be returning the following week.

Leah and the kids had surprised him by stopping off at the park to watch the last couple of innings. Damn but it felt good to hear Leah cheering for him from the stands. In all the time he'd known his sister-in-law, Paul couldn't recall ever hearing her raise her voice. He'd played his best when Leah and the kids were there, and afterward, for a treat, he'd taken everyone out to McDonald's for burgers.

The afternoon gave him no clue to the origin of his rotten mood, either. Everything had gone exceptionally well. He was able to repair the screen in Kelsey's bedroom without a hitch. He'd even had time to mow the lawn. The twins had followed behind him with their plastic mowers, blowing bubbles into the bright June sunshine. They'd laughed and raced after the dandelion seeds Paul blew into the wind.

Leah was in the backyard with Kelsey, planting the herbs she had picked up at the local nursery. She'd never grown them before and wanted to see how well they did. He had teased her about her green thumb, and the sound of her laughter had lingered with him long after he'd gone into the house.

Before he knew it, dinner was on the table and Leah was getting ready for her date with Bill Mullins. Paul had tried to be cool about it, nonchalant. He was happy she was going out, wasn't he? Hell, making sure her social life continued was the least he could do to be sure she got away from the daily grind of looking after the house and the kids.

Bill looked like a decent enough guy. A bit on the boring side, but then he hadn't expected a college professor to have the personality of a stand-up comedian.

Once the kids were down and asleep, Paul went into his den and turned on the computer to work on his novel. It was the first time in months that he'd had the opportunity to take some uninterrupted time for himself.

He should be happy. Overjoyed.

But he wasn't.

He found himself brooding, his attention span short, his thoughts on everything but what they should have been on—his novel. He worked late, forcing himself to review the five chapters he'd written before Kelsey was born.

It was well past eleven when he finished reading. The novel was good. At least he thought it was, but what the hell did he know? Pretty damn little, he decided.

He didn't have any reason to delay going to bed, but was strangely reluctant to do so. The boys would be awake before six, Paul knew. He had told them to crawl into bed with him when they awoke and let Leah sleep.

He checked and found the kids sleeping soundly, and then glanced at his watch, wondering how much longer Leah would be out. She hadn't told him what time she'd be back, and he hadn't asked.

He sat down in the living room with a novel he'd been wanting to read, but his mind kept wandering from the written page. The image of Bill taking Leah in his arms and kissing her saturated his mind.

The fury that claimed him took Paul by storm. He slammed the book shut and stood abruptly, his chest heaving with exertion. If Bill was kissing Leah, it wasn't any of his damn business. It shouldn't matter to him.

Knotting his fist at his side, he sank back down into the chair and opened the book a second time. It did little good. The anger simmered just below the surface, looking for an excuse to erupt...only there wasn't anyone around to pick a fight with except himself.

He was going to stay awake and wait for her, Paul decided. He didn't care how late she was; he was going to sit right in this chair until she was home. If she didn't come home...well, he'd deal with that when the time came. He would need to do some serious thinking if it turned out Leah spent the night with Bill Mullins. He didn't want an immoral woman raising his children.

Leah, immoral? Paul wanted to kick himself. He'd never known anyone more honest and forthright.

A car door closing sounded from the front of the house, and Paul's heart went into a panic. He leapt off the chair as if he'd been caught doing something illegal. If Leah invited Bill inside, he didn't want them to think he was purposely waiting up for her.

Retreating to his bedroom and turning off the lights wouldn't work, either. They would have already noticed the lamp on in the living-room.

Thinking quickly, Paul raced into Kelsey's bedroom. Careful so as not to wake her, he picked her up from the crib and hurried back to his chair, holding his small sleeping daughter in his arms.

He'd been seated no more than a couple of seconds when Leah quietly slipped inside the house. She paused when she saw him and Kelsey, and immediately looked concerned.

"Is she sick? I knew I shouldn't have left her when she was teething." The concern in her voice was like a soothing balm, easing Paul's loathsome temper. He glanced down on the slumbering infant and brushed the wisps of blond hair from her temple. If Kelsey had been teething, he hadn't known it. She'd been a perfect baby all evening.

"She's been fussy all week," Leah said, looking as if she felt guilty for leaving her.

"Kelsey's fine...now," Paul said, gently placing his sleeping daughter over his shoulder and patting her back. He felt like a fool playing this game with Leah, but he hadn't the courage to tell her the truth. Paul had rarely felt more like a heel. "I was just getting ready to put her back to bed."

"Was she up all night fussing?"

"Not at all," he was quick to assure her, hating himself for the deception.

"I could use a cup of tea," Leah said, hanging her sweater in the hall closet. "How about you?"

"That sounds good," he answered in a whisper. He carried Kelsey back to her bedroom and gently placed her facedown in the crib.

When he returned to the kitchen, Leah had set the teakettle on the burner and was bringing down two mugs.

She looked good this evening, Paul mused, burying his hands in his pockets as he watched her graceful movements. She looked...he searched for the right word. Beautiful, he decided. For reasons he couldn't explain, he'd never thought of Leah in those terms before. She possessed a rare beauty a man could get lost in. She turned to smile at him, and he found himself hopelessly lost in the fathomless depth of her eyes. Lost in her wistfully intriguing smile.

Leah swallowed and looked away.

Paul pulled himself from his trance and walked around to the other side of the kitchen, opening the refrigerator and taking out the milk. He didn't generally drink his tea with milk, but he needed an excuse to walk away from her and that one conveniently presented itself.

"I was just thinking," he said, setting the milk carton in the center of the table.

"Oh?"

"You should marry Bill." Paul wouldn't have surprised himself more had he suggested they jump off the Tacoma Narrows Bridge. It was the last thing he wanted. It would be disastrous to the children if Leah were to leave now. Disastrous to him too.

"Marry Bill?" she echoed, astonished.

"He seems the nice sort." He would sound like a fool if he claimed the suggestion had been a joke. Given no other option, he took his own stupid idea even further.

"Bill's not the marrying kind," she explained.

"Why not?"

She shrugged. "He's been married once before, and apparently it was a bad experience."

"What about you, Leah?" Paul didn't know why he couldn't leave the subject alone. He didn't know why he felt the need to press it again and again, when it was the very thing he dreaded most.

"What about me?"

"You should be married." For reasons he couldn't begin to explain, it felt strangely comforting to have the subject out in the open. He'd never understood why Leah hadn't married. She was generous. Unselfish. Gentle. He'd watched her with the children all these months, and thanked God with every breath he drew that she was there with him.

At the question Leah cast him a surprised look. "I guess I'm a lot like Bill. I'm not the marrying kind."

"I don't buy that."

She carried the steeping tea to the table and filled their mugs. Pulling out her chair, she sat down. "I've never been in love."

"Why not?"

Leah laughed, the sound of her laughter sweet and gentle. "I don't know. It just never happened."

"What about Bill?"

She shook her head. "I couldn't ever see myself in love with Bill. He's too self-involved. I can't see us being anything more than just friends."

"Did you have a good time this evening?"

"Fair." She lowered her gaze, and Paul thought he might have detected a blush. "I . . . I don't think I'll be seeing Bill again." She said it as if she expected an argument from him.

"Why not?"

"Because . . . I have my reasons. Do you mind if we drop the subject?"

"Sure, I mean . . . no, I don't mind. I don't mean to pry." The dark mood that had been pressing down on him all evening mysteriously lifted. Paul didn't want to analyze his feelings, at least not then. He hadn't wanted to say anything to Leah earlier, but he wasn't that keen on her fellow professor. Pressed for specifics, he couldn't have defined his feelings, other than that he simply didn't have a good feeling about the other man.

"How did everything go with the kids tonight?" Leah asked in a blatant effort to change the subject.

"Good. They all went down without a problem."

"Did Ryan take his blankie to bed with him?"

Paul chuckled. "He made a gallant effort to go without it, but in the end he succumbed."

Leah grinned and, leaning back in her chair, she sipped her tea. "I suspect if Ryan took his blankie to bed with him then Ronnie considered it his God-given right to suck his thumb."

"Naturally." Paul smiled and sipped his own tea. "I had a chance to work on my novel this evening." He wasn't sure why he mentioned his book to Leah. He'd given up analyzing the things he said. He only knew it was something he'd intended to tell her.

"How's it coming?"

He grinned a bit sheepishly. "Better than I thought it was."

"How far are you into it?"

"Five chapters . . . a hundred and ten pages, to be exact."

"What's it about?"

Her interest seemed genuine; otherwise Paul wouldn't have bored her with the plot line. The story had been brewing in his mind long before he'd decided to write it down. It had come out of his experience in Alaska. An espionage story that involved Russia and the Middle East. The basic World War III nightmare.

Leah listened intently. Then asked him several thought-provoking questions. Paul answered them as best he could, amazed at her insights. Grateful, too, because she pointed out a major plot weakness he'd overlooked.

The next time he glanced at his watch it was nearly one. Paul was astonished. They'd been talking for more than an hour and a half.

"My goodness," Leah said, noting the time herself. "I had no idea it was so late."

"Me, either."

They both stood and moved toward the sink. Leah put her cup down first, then Paul followed. But when she turned, apparently she didn't realize he was directly behind her. In an effort to keep from colliding with him, she jerked back.

Paul's arms instinctively reached out to steady her. His hands closed over her shoulders.

They both froze.

For a long moment neither moved. Paul's eyes drifted slowly over Leah's flushed features. Her arms were raised, her hands braced against the solid wall of his chest. He noted the gentle thrust of her breasts. Small and proud...just the right size to fill a man's palms.

He shouldn't be thinking such things, Paul realized, mentally chastising himself.

"Are you all right?" he asked once he found his voice. Emotion thickened the air until he could neither breathe nor think. All he seemed capable of was feeling. Once more he marveled at her beauty, and the power that swept through him holding her so gently in his embrace.

"I'm fine." Her words were scarcely audible, and she was slightly breathless. Her eyes continued to hold his.

Her breath fled.

Paul's followed. He knew he should release her. He knew he had held on to her much longer than necessary. He knew...dear God, help him, he knew he was going to kiss her.

Before he could stop himself, before the iron control slipped back into place, Paul lowered his mouth to hers.

Desire and guilt waged a fierce battle within him. He wanted this kiss, wanted it more passionately than he could ever remember wanting anything. It had been so long since he'd tasted a woman. So very long...

The hunger had never been this raw. Paul claimed her lips, and when she sighed and opened to him, he probed her mouth with his tongue.

"Oh, God," Paul prayed silently, "help me . . . help me."

But God, apparently, was occupied somewhere else.

Chapter Five

Paul felt as though someone had carved out his insides. He felt empty...no, he corrected himself, it wasn't an emptiness he was experiencing, but he couldn't define the wide range of emotions that raged through him.

He abruptly dropped his arms, releasing Leah. Wordlessly they stepped away from each other. He noted how swollen her lips were, how moist. Her beautiful, multifaceted eyes were wide and staring up at him.

He wanted to tell her he was sorry, beg her forgiveness, but he couldn't make himself do it. She looked at him, unblinking, her features devoid of color.

Then, just when he was about to find the courage to talk to her, she edged her way past him and hurried down the hallway to her bedroom. The sound of her door closing echoed like a gunshot in the night.

Paul thought to follow her, to explain, only he didn't know what he could say that would possibly excuse what he'd done. He waited a few minutes until he could control the trembling in his hands, and then turned off the lights and headed down the hallway to his own room.

Outside Leah's door he hesitated. Knotting his fists at his sides, he silently berated himself for not knowing what to do. What to say. Or how to say it.

He'd known he was going to kiss her in plenty of time to stop himself, yet he hadn't. He'd given in to the impulse, knowing full well he'd be left to deal with the regrets later. None of that had mattered at the time. He'd wanted to taste her. He'd *needed* to taste her.

He'd pulled her into his arms, meshing her body with his. Her nipples had pearled and flirted with his chest, adding to the pleasure.

Adding to his guilt.

Her right hand had moved up from his chest to caress his face. How warm her fingers had felt against the coolness of his skin. How smooth.

How right.

It was then that he'd deepened the kiss, using the tip of his tongue to part the seam of her lips, and when she'd given a small gasp—Paul didn't know if it was from pleasure or surprise—he'd slipped his tongue forward to meet hers.

Whatever control Paul possessed, which admittedly was damn little, had been lost at that moment. He'd plowed his hands into her hair and hungrily slanted his mouth over hers, opening wider and wider, wanting to possess more and more of her.

He couldn't make himself break away. Couldn't make himself *want* to break away. Her tongue had shyly darted forward, and they'd danced and played with one another until everything had gone completely out of his control.

The kiss turned deep, and, heaven help him, savage. Paul had wanted to consume her and would have, he feared, if she hadn't twisted slightly and rubbed herself against the throbbing heat of his arousal. In that moment Paul knew it had to end before the fire of his need burned out of control.

He tore his mouth from hers. They were both gasping for breath, their shoulders heaving. The look on Leah's sweet face would haunt him to the grave.

He read her shock. Her confusion. But what hurt the most was the self-loathing he saw. Perhaps what he was viewing in her eyes was a reflection of what was in his own. Paul didn't know anymore.

Defeated, he moved past her bedroom door, followed by the taunting demons of guilt and desire. It hurt to walk away from Leah. Mentally and physically. It had been nearly nine months since he'd found the physical release a woman's body afforded him. Nine hellish, nightmare-filled months.

But that was no excuse. He wasn't some teenager fighting hormones. He was fast approaching forty; one would assume that by now he'd have his libido under control.

Was it so wrong to feel again? he asked himself as he readied for bed.

Yes, came the immediate response. He had known, he had accepted it, when Diane had died. That portion of his life was finished. Gone forever. He'd shared a healthy, active sex life with his wife, and when she died he couldn't imagine himself ever wanting another woman. But perhaps he'd been shortsighted. Perhaps he'd been foolish. He was still alive. Needy.

But Leah? His wife's sister?

He rubbed a hand down his face.

She'd felt so warm. She'd tasted so sweet ... so womanly. And alive.

Alive.

The word seared itself into Paul's mind.

He felt trapped.

Diane was gone. Dead. He was alive. But was he? He felt caught somewhere between life and death. One foot in the present and the other in the past.

Diane and Leah.

Sweet heaven, *they were sisters*. He was related to Leah. How could he feel the way he did for her? It was wrong. Dead wrong.

Yet for the first time since he'd lost Diane, he felt vitally alive.

A sharp, crystal-clear memory of his wife drifted into his mind. It was the day she'd learned she was pregnant with Kelsey. She had planned a surprise celebration of the news for when he returned home from work. Leah had taken the boys to the movies, giving him and Diane several uninterrupted hours. They'd made love and then sat up in bed eating ice cream and pickles. The memory of the teasing and the laughter would stay with him all his life. He'd loved his wife.

Loved her more than life itself. But he was the one left behind in the world. The one dealing with reality.

The image of Diane sitting in their bed, ice cream smeared across her mouth, faded. Paul squeezed his eyes closed as tightly as he could, trying unsuccessfully to bring her back. Instead it was Leah who drifted into his mind. Leah, sitting in the sunshine while working in the garden. The children were gathered around her, Kelsey trying to catch a gold-winged butterfly, his sons busy digging in the dirt.

Dear God, what had he done? The fact that he'd inflicted himself upon Leah filled him with a vengeful self-directed anger. Heaven only knew what he was going to say to her in the morning.

What the hell could he say? He didn't have a single excuse to offer her. A single explanation to give. Needing her this way, using her this way, had been selfish and wrong.

But right, his mind countered. Nothing had ever felt more right.

Wrong. Wrong. Wrong.

Dear heaven, he was so confused. His thoughts were muddier than the Mississippi River.

Paul didn't know what he was going to do.

Leah couldn't sleep. She lay on her back staring toward the ceiling in the darkened room. Silent tears slipped from the corners of her eyes, rolling into her hair and onto her pillow. She let them fall, knowing it would do no good to try to stop the pent-up emotion.

She hadn't known kissing could be so good. She hadn't known desire could burn so hot. She'd always been so sensible when it came to men and relationships. In charge of every situation. Always in control.

Until Paul had kissed her. One kiss and her body had felt as if it were on fire, empty and aching.

Her heart was beating much too fast, its cadence echoing in her ear. Her body throbbed with pleasure.

With shame.

With need.

If only Paul had said something. But she'd seen the stricken look in his eyes, seen for herself his tortured regret. Knowing what he felt hurt her more than anything since Diane's death. Unable to bear it any longer, Leah had turned, with as much dignity as she could muster, and retreated to her bedroom.

But her dignity was cold comfort. Her heart was heavy, weighing down her chest.

If only she knew what had prompted Paul to kiss her. Had she, without realizing it, done or said something to lead him on, sent out silent messages to him, seeking his touch?

She must have; otherwise she wouldn't have gone so eagerly into his arms. Otherwise she would have broken away. It was all too clear how willingly she'd accepted his embrace.

Mortified by the thought, she covered her face with her hands, the heat of her embarrassment warming her palms.

Leah shivered, remembering the way she'd blatantly responded to him. Her head was swirling. She'd opened up to Paul. Opened her arms. Opened her heart. And...her face grew hotter still. She'd been looking for more. Much more.

She'd lost herself in his kiss, responding to him as she never had to another man. Oh God, she had actually pressed herself hard against him—at the hip, no less. Needing him so desperately, she'd behaved like a wanton.

The kiss had gone wild, and the fire and demand had shot through her veins like molten lava. For the first time in her life, Leah had felt completely out of control with a man. Sweet heaven, she'd wanted him. Wanted to feel his arms around her. Wanted to taste his kiss. Wanted to experience the welcoming touch of his tongue as it boldly stroked hers.

She'd wanted her sister's husband.

Leah squeezed her eyes closed and waited for the revulsion to attack her senses. For the overwhelming load of guilt to bury her in its mire.

She waited. And waited.

But it didn't come.

Yet in her heart of hearts, Leah experienced such regret that it all but consumed her. Regret and need made for one hell of a combination.

Was she falling in love with Paul? Leah asked herself.

She couldn't answer that any more than she could answer any of the other questions that plagued her, demanding a response.

Her fingers explored her still-swollen lips. They felt bruised...just like her heart. The memory of those brief moments in his arms returned, bringing with it all the fever, all the madness, all the fury of their kiss.

She shouldn't be feeling these things, she chastised herself mentally. It was wrong. She couldn't allow herself to feel any of this toward Paul.

Leah didn't know how she was going to look him in the eye come morning. She didn't know how she was going to be able to pretend nothing had happened.

Around her the night breathed. The dark closed in. The rain, which had been threatening all evening, hammered against the windows.

It was a long time before she fell asleep.

Leah woke the following morning, feeling as though she hadn't slept at all. The boys were awake; she could hear them in the kitchen with Paul. Apparently Kelsey was up and about, as well. She rolled onto her side and glanced at her clock radio. It was nearly nine. How Paul had been able to keep the kids from waking her was a mystery. Throwing back the covers, she hurried out of bed and quickly dressed for church.

"Leah," Ronnie cried when she walked into the kitchen, "Ryan got the prize in the cereal box. Tell Daddy it's my turn."

"I don't remember whose turn it is," she told him, surprised to see that both boys and Kelsey were already dressed.

"It's my turn," Ronnie insisted.

"Ryan can share." Paul's gruff voice wasn't any comfort. Thus far Leah had been able to avoid looking at him, but she wouldn't be able to keep it up much longer.

He hadn't spoken directly to her, which didn't help ease the tension between them. Leah could feel the strained nervousness as profoundly as she had felt his touch the night before.

She poured herself a cup of coffee and hurried into the bathroom where she applied her makeup. By the time she'd finished, Paul had set the breakfast dishes in the dishwasher and wiped off the table.

Leah half expected him to make an excuse for not attending church services with her that morning. She was half hoping he would. Apparently Paul felt the need to talk to God as strongly as she did, because he didn't offer any excuse to stay home.

They didn't exchange a word on the short drive to the church. Even the children were strangely quiet.

Once they arrived, Leah delivered Kelsey to the nursery, while Paul escorted the boys to their Sunday school class.

When Leah entered the sanctuary, she noted Paul's parents had arrived and, sighing with relief, opted to sit with them. Rich and Jamie sat in the pew directly in front of them. Leah felt comforted being surrounded by Paul's family.

When Paul slipped into the seat next to her, she noted how he maintained a safe distance between them.

The worship service passed in a blur for Leah. Her head was so full of what had happened between her and Paul that she couldn't concentrate on the sermon.

When they stood for the singing of the closing hymn, Elizabeth Manning leaned toward Leah and whispered, "Are you feeling all right?"

Leah quickly nodded.

"You're looking pale. Paul is, too."

"I'm fine." But her heart was hammering at how easily Elizabeth had detected the tension between her and Paul. She could only pray that her alarm didn't show in her eyes.

As they finished singing the final verse of the hymn, Leah felt Paul's gaze searching out hers. Everything in her wanted to turn and look at him, but she lacked the courage. Eventually they would need to say something to one another. Eventually they were going to have to discuss what had happened. But she wasn't ready now and she didn't know how long it would take her before she was.

Leah met Jamie, Rich's wife, on the way into the nursery to pick up Kelsey. "You're coming, aren't you?" she asked. At Leah's blank look, Jamie elaborated. "Mom wants us all to come over for brunch. No doubt Paul neglected to tell you."

"Ah . . ."

"Typical man," Jamie said with a soft smile. "How's everything working out?"

"Great," Leah responded with a too-bright smile. She had only talked to Paul's sister-in-law a handful of times, but she enjoyed Jamie, found her friendly and undemanding. Bethany, Jamie and Rich's little girl, was nearly eighteen months old now and, from something Paul had said, it looked as if the couple would be having a second child soon.

Paul met Leah in the hallway outside the nursery. "Mom and Dad invited us over to brunch. Is that all right with you?"

"It's fine." They were the first words he'd spoken to her all morning and they sounded stilted and distant.

"If you'd rather, I could drop you off at the house and take the kids over myself."

The suggestion hurt—he was looking to avoid her company—but she tried not to let it show. "It'd...only raise questions if I didn't come."

"You're sure?"

She shifted a squirming Kelsey in her arms. "If you'd prefer me not to be there, just say so." Her eyes defiantly met his.

"I want you there," he admitted, then turned and left her.

In retrospect Leah realized she should have taken Paul up on his offer to drop her off at the house. The brunch was trying for both of them. Although they attempted to disguise the tension, Leah knew they did a poor job.

After they'd gathered up the kids, the elder Mannings walked them out to the car. They didn't say anything. They didn't have to. It was apparent in the worried look in their eyes and the lack of conversation.

All three of the children fell asleep in the car on the ride home. Leah carried in Kelsey, while Paul dealt with the boys. She was on her way out of the nursery, headed toward her own room to take a nap herself, when Paul stopped her.

"We have to talk," he announced starkly.

Leah nervously shifted her weight, her heart pounding with dread. She wasn't ready. Yet she knew they couldn't delay a confrontation much longer.

"I don't know where to start," he said after an awkward moment.

Leah said nothing. She didn't know where to start, either. A sense of heady relief that he was willing to bring everything into the open filled her. With it came a sense of regret, too, over the fact that it was even necessary.

"I didn't mean for it to happen," he said, his anger buried just below the surface of his words. "I certainly didn't plan it, if that's what you're thinking."

"I... realized that."

"I know I frightened you."

"No." She couldn't very well tell him that their kissing was one of the most beautiful experiences of her life. She couldn't very well admit that she'd never felt in any man's arms the things she had with him.

"I didn't?" He seemed surprised to learn that. He hesitated and then, plowing his fingers through his hair, he turned abruptly and moved away from her. "I...I don't know what came over me. I love Diane...I haven't been with another woman since..."

At the mention of her sister's name, Leah went stiff. The implication nearly choked her, and her heart sank to her knees. "In other words you were...horny...and I just happened to be handy."

"No." The lone word was practically shouted. "God, no. It wasn't that at all."

"Then what was it?"

"If I knew that, do you think I'd be putting us through this hell?" he demanded. "I didn't kiss just any woman. It was you. I'm attracted to *you*, Leah." He made it sound like a confession, one that would convict him of a malicious crime. "I don't know when it happened, or even how. I suspect it's only natural, the two of us living here the way we do."

"I don't buy that."

"Why the hell not? I'm trying to be as honest and as objective as I know how to be."

"I know," she breathed softly.

"Then what don't you buy?"

When it came right down to it, Leah couldn't believe that Paul could possibly find her attractive after having loved Diane. Leah knew her assets well, and captivating men wasn't one of them. She had learned early in life she couldn't compete with her sister. She hadn't ever wanted to. Paul had loved Diane. And having loved a woman who was laughter and sunshine and beauty, it wasn't likely he'd appreciate a woman who was sensible and dull.

But she couldn't find the words to explain this to Paul.

"I... think it might be best if we both put the incident behind us and go on as before," she said after an awkward silence.

"That doesn't answer my question."

"I don't want to talk about it," she insisted, raising her voice.

Her fervor seemed to surprise him. "In other words you want to forget it ever happened?"

"Yes."

He eyed her skeptically. "Can you?"

"Yes," she lied. "Can't you?"

He hesitated, then abruptly nodded. "It goes without saying, it won't happen again. You have my word on it."

Paul knew he'd badly blundered talking to Leah. Seeing her that morning, watching the way her eyes kept avoiding his, ate at his soul like acid. With everything in him, he wanted to take her hands in his and plead for her forgiveness. But when he finally had built up the courage to confront her, he'd done it all wrong. He'd made it sound as though he'd kissed her because he had gone nearly a year without sexual gratification and she was available, within reach.

He hadn't even told her how sorry he was.

But was he?

Paul didn't know anymore. He'd woken and his arms had felt empty without her. The need to hold her again burned through him. For long seconds he lay there, his heart racing.

He waited for guilt to slap him across the face. For Diane's image to appear and damn him for his weakness. For God to intervene and save him from himself.

It didn't happen.

Heaven help him, all Paul could think about was how much he wanted to kiss Leah again.

Her reaction in the morning quickly convinced him that his actions had betrayed a basic trust between them. She was embarrassed, perhaps even frightened. He had known that he was going to need to assure her. He should have done it immediately upon her waking. But he'd delayed it, promising himself he'd do it right after church. Then they'd gotten trapped in the invitation to his parents' house, and the delay had only made it more difficult. More awkward.

During the ride home he'd mentally rehearsed everything he planned to say. It had sounded good in his mind, but the minute he'd gone to voice his thoughts, he'd botched everything.

What else could he do but promise never to touch her again? It was all too apparent he'd offended her. His hungry need had repulsed her.

Leah napped well into the afternoon. When she woke, Paul was closed up in his den, working on his novel, she presumed. He didn't come out until it was dinnertime, and only then long enough to dish up his plate, eat and quickly retreat again.

After bath time Leah read to the boys until they were sleepy and her voice had grown hoarse. Once the kids were tucked away, she withdrew into her bedroom and read late into the night.

By the time she woke in the morning, Paul had already left for the office.

The boys requested Eggs McManning for breakfast. By now Leah was quite proficient at assembling the family favorite. She was standing in front of the stove, the spatula in her hand, when the tears filled her eyes. They came so unexpectedly that she was caught completely unaware. She brushed them aside, hoping the twins wouldn't notice.

What in heaven's name did she have to be weeping about? Leah didn't know. Was it that she was falling in love with a man who could never love her back? That she lay awake nights remembering how hot and greedy his mouth had felt over her own? That she dare not look him in the eye for fear he'd be able to read what she felt? Leah could hardly remember being more miserable in her life.

Paul let himself in the house and was met by the enticing smells of dinner. He walked unnoticed into the kitchen and stopped, mesmerized by the sight of Leah standing at the stove. He'd purposely avoided her that morning, left early just so he wouldn't have to smile and pretend nothing had changed between them. He never had been much good at pretending. His expertise was in escape, so he'd left early. Now he doubted the wisdom of his actions.

The impact of seeing Leah, of being this close to her after nearly twenty-four hours, hit him hard. It was as though he'd been physically punched, his lungs emptied of air. He didn't know how he could have been so blind all these weeks. Blind to her beauty, blind to his own feelings.

He must have made some sound because Leah turned abruptly around to face him. "I didn't hear you come in," she said as normally as always.

Paul was slowly going out of his mind, and she was frying pork chops as if there wasn't a thing wrong. He had to marvel at her ability to pretend. To him the tension was thick enough to slice into bite-sized pieces.

Dear God, maybe it was all him. Maybe she didn't feel it. Maybe he was the only one.

The thought wasn't comforting.

Paul didn't realize his mistake until they were finished with dinner. Leah had said very little. The boys were crabby; Paul blamed it on the tension between him and Leah. She almost fooled him, almost convinced him. By heaven, she gave an award-winning performance. He had to marvel at her ability.

Yet he said nothing. How could he? Like her, he was trapped into pretending.

It rained that night, beating hard against his window in a relentless rhythm. For the third night in a row, Paul found it difficult to sleep. The howling wind wasn't helping matters any.

He thought about getting up, drinking a glass of milk. Maybe even reading for a while. Of course he could revert to pacing away the long hours until morning, the way he'd done the first few months after Diane had died.

What was really bothering him was Leah. Knowing she was so close. Only two doors away. His body reacted almost immediately to thoughts of her snuggled up in bed, her lush body warm and inviting.

His breath quickened as the evidence of his desire came to taunt him. All on the backlash of guilt. Dear God, it was happening all over again. What kind of sick man was he? Wanting his sister-in-law? Needing her so desperately.

Night. Wind. Rain. Wanting Leah. Loving Diane. Suddenly it all became too much for him, and he impatiently tossed aside the blankets and climbed out of bed. Bare-chested he walked into the kitchen and opened the refrigerator. He poured himself a glass of milk and drank it down in three gulps. Rinsing out the glass, he set it in the sink and headed down the hallway to his room.

A movement in the shadows caught his attention.

"Leah?"

"Paul?"

"What are you doing up?"

"I . . . couldn't sleep. I was just going to get myself a glass of milk."

His eyes quickly adjusted to the dark. As soon as they did, Paul wished they hadn't. She stood in the shadows, but the pale light coming from the night-light in the twins' bedroom silhouetted her lithe form, highlighting her lush breasts and the slimness of her waist and hips. She was slight, much smaller than he'd realized. A man would need to be cautious when making love to her. Of fitting his body into hers . . . Paul nearly groaned out loud as he deliberately forced the image from his mind.

"Why are you up?" she asked, sounding breathless and unsure.

"I couldn't sleep, either."

It was probably his imagination, but Paul could have sworn the oxygen supply in the hallway had decreased. His heart pounded so loud he feared she'd hear it.

The silence lingered to embarrassing proportions, yet neither moved. The past few days had been miserable ones for Paul. Lonely days. Troubled days.

"I . . . had a glass of milk myself," he offered after a few timeless moments, and was genuinely surprised by how difficult it was to speak coherently.

The desire to touch her was suddenly so strong he had to knot his fists at his sides in order to resist reaching for her. The need to savor her softness drained what little strength he possessed.

Her voice was little more than a trembling whisper when she spoke. "The storm . . . kept me awake." She looked up at him, her eyes wide and imploring.

Wanting.

Neither moved. Neither breathed.

Paul groaned inwardly. Didn't she know the signals she was sending him?

Apparently not. His control was stretched hair thin, as it was; this was too much. But he held on to it, because the hard truth of the matter was, he didn't know if she had an inkling of what she was doing, staring up at him with her eyes wide and pleading.

"I should be getting back to bed," he suggested.

"Yes."

They were so close her breath fanned his face. By rotating his chin he was able to slowly caress the top of her head. How silky smooth her hair felt. How clean and fresh. He closed his eyes and breathed in the womanly scent of her.

Leah lifted her face so their lips were mere inches apart. Their breaths coming in soft gasps. Needy gasps. He relished the feel of her breath so close to his face.

"Leah...dear God." The words came deep from his throat in a tight groan. "Stop me," he pleaded, not sure she'd even be able to decipher his words.

He was a hairbreadth from taking her in his arms, of breaking his promise to himself. His promise to the memory of his dead wife, his promise to God, but most important, his promise to Leah.

Chapter Six

Paul didn't know how he managed to avoid kissing Leah. He stumbled back to his room and literally fell across his bed. He listened and heard her return to her bedroom, and only then was he able to breathe easily.

He'd expected to encounter so many problems when Leah had moved in with him and the children, but having to fight a strong sexual attraction to her hadn't once entered his mind.

Who would have believed something like this would happen? Not Paul.

It had all started with a simple kiss. An anything-but-simple kiss, he amended. He would gladly surrender everything he owned not to have touched her that first time. Not to have tasted her sweetness, her willingness. Not to know how soft her body felt in his arms, how delicate and special.

One kiss had brought him far past the point of pleasure; it had opened a Pandora's box of hungry need. A need that threatened to consume him.

His desire for her was shameless. Only a few minutes earlier it had taken every bit of control he possessed to walk away from her. Frankly he didn't know if he'd have the strength to do it again.

Where the hell did that leave them?

Paul didn't know what had come over him the past few days. Although he was nearly thirty when he had married Diane, he hadn't had a broad history of sexual experience. He wasn't the type of man who had women beating down his door. His army buddies had bragged about their sexual conquests and playfully joked with Paul, claiming he was the only man they knew who was more interested in a woman's mind than her bustline.

Not so with Leah. He'd been fighting erotic fantasies about her for days, doggedly chasing them out of his mind, and damning himself for his thoughts.

His body felt as though it were on fire, aching and wanting. For years he had prided himself on his self-control, his discipline, but lately that discipline was breaking down. In fact it was quickly going to hell in a hand basket, as the saying went.

Although his breathing calmed, the frightening excitement didn't lessen once Paul was in his own room; if anything, it increased. Every time he closed his eyes, Leah was there, looking up at him, her beautiful eyes languid with desire. Every instinct he had wanted to take her in his arms and press her tightly against him, let her know the power she held over him. He longed to fit his hands at her waist and nestle close to her womanly softness. He wanted her to rub herself against him the way she had that fateful night. He longed to touch her breasts, take her nipples in his mouth and love her... oh, dear God, it was happening all over again.

He didn't know what he was going to do. He'd already discovered he couldn't ignore her. He couldn't be in the same room and not experience the throbbing tension between them. No matter how hard he tried, he couldn't keep the memories of the night he'd kissed her from bombarding his mind. No more than he could keep the guilt at bay for feeling the things he did.

Paul didn't know how Leah could pretend this strained awareness didn't exist between them. She did a masterful job of it, but the skill was beyond him.

He could do what he'd done that very morning— leaving for work early in order to avoid any contact, verbal or otherwise, with her. But the problem with that was his children. He couldn't escape Leah without depriving himself of what little time he had with them. In the end he'd only be cheating himself.

The one other option that presented itself was an open, honest discussion. He'd attempted that once and had badly blundered the whole thing.

Try as he might, Paul couldn't come up with a tactful way of saying he wanted to take her to bed with him, and would she kindly forgive him if he said or did anything that indicated as much.

Paul rubbed a hand down his face. He was much worse off than he had thought. Quite simply he didn't know what the hell he was going to do.

* * *

"Your parents phoned." That was how Leah greeted Paul when he returned home from work the following evening. Just the way she said it alerted him to the fact that she'd had a bad day herself. He was almost glad. His own had been a disaster, and if she'd been miserable, too, then all the better.

His mood lightened considerably.

"Is something wrong?"

Leah shrugged, keeping her back to him—an irritating habit of late. "They asked if they could come visit."

"What did you tell them?"

Hearing his father, Ryan raced from the backyard into the kitchen, and Paul lifted his son into his arms, hugging him briefly.

"What could I say?" Leah continued, turning to face him. "I told them they were welcome any time."

Ronnie raced in behind his brother, looking for the customary hug. Paul absently complied, then bent over and kissed Kelsey's chubby cheek as she gleefully pounded away on a kettle with a wooden spoon.

"They wanted to be sure we were both going to be home."

Paul straightened slowly. "That sounds ominous."

"I... think it might be." Leah turned back to the counter where she was grating cheese for a taco salad.

Paul reached over and stole a black olive from the bed of lettuce. "What makes you say that?"

"Your mother sensed something was wrong... between us Sunday morning," she explained tightly.

"So?" It surprised Paul that he could sound so nonchalant about the whole thing. He was feeling anything but this devil-may-care charade he was acting out. Not that he was worried about his parents' visit.

"So... it worries me."

"Why?"

She turned and glared at him, and it was all Paul could do not to clap his hands and cry out, "Hot damn!" Finally. Finally. Leah Baker was showing some emotion. She couldn't pretend anymore. She couldn't ignore him any longer. Couldn't continue this maddening game of pretend.

His parents arrived shortly after seven-thirty. The kitchen was clean, and the boys were outside playing on the swing set in the mid-June sun. Kelsey had been diapered and fed and put down for the night. Paul had to marvel, not for the first time, at Leah's efficiency.

The minute he stepped in the house his father's gaze sought out Paul's. There was something on his mind, all right. Paul knew the look. It was one Eric Manning wore when he was worried about something. When a problem was weighing heavily on his mind. The last time Paul could remember seeing his father wearing that particular facial expression was when Christy had announced she was married to Cody Franklin. The news came as one hell of a shock, especially since she was engaged to James Wilkens at the time. Leave it to his youngest sister to be married to one man while engaged to another.

"Something's troubling you, Dad?" Paul asked, wondering at his father's mood.

"I'd like to talk to you."

"Sure."

Eric sent an apologetic look to Leah. "Privately, if you don't mind?"

"Of course not." Paul sent Leah a glance, too. Her eyes were seeking out his, and she looked so uncertain, so dubious, that he had to resist an urge to tell her there was nothing to worry about. But he said nothing, because he wasn't sure himself.

"And while you two are chatting, Leah and I can have some time to ourselves," his mother said, conversationally enough. Only Paul wasn't fooled. He knew that tone of voice. It was the same one his mother used when he was a boy and he'd done something that worried her. She wasn't angry, just concerned. That concern often led to having the car keys taken away from him, or grounding him until his thinking aligned with that of his parents.

Whatever was going on sounded fateful. Leah, who had apparently recovered, cast him a prim I-told-you-so expression and led the way into the kitchen.

Paul hadn't a clue what was going on, but he was pretty sure he didn't like it. His parents were wonderful. The first six months after Kelsey was born, Paul couldn't have survived emotionally without their support and encouragement. But he was thirty-six years old, far past the point of being reprimanded by them.

Leah claimed his parents had sensed something was awry between the two of them last Sunday. Personally Paul doubted that. Yes, matters had been a bit strained and his family might have read something into it, but surely that hadn't brought about this unexpected visit.

Paul led his father into the den and closed the door. The room wasn't large, but adequate. His desk and computer took up one entire wall. Two more walls were dominated by bookshelves. Paul gave his father his desk chair and took the stool for himself.

"Is something wrong, Dad?"

"Not really." As he spoke, he slowly raised his eyes to meet Paul's. "At least I hope not."

Paul smiled benignly, and waited.

"As you know, your mother and I are leaving early next week for Montana. She's got her heart set on being with Christy for the birth of this baby."

"Yes, I know. You don't need to worry about the house. Jason, Rich and I will look after the old homestead for you."

"It's not the house I'm worried about," the elder Manning stated gruffly, with a dash of impatience.

"Then what is it?"

"It's Leah."

Paul went stiff. So much for all the reassurances he'd been feeding himself. His father was staring at him as though he expected Paul to leap up and announce he was lusting after her. God knew it was close enough to the truth.

"What about Leah?" Paul asked once he could be certain his voice wouldn't portray his uneasiness.

"I'm concerned about her."

It went without saying that Leah worked too hard. She didn't take nearly enough time for herself. Diane had been far more social than Leah, more outgoing. Leah's idea of treating herself was sitting down and reading a good book.

"Your family realizes everything's on the up-and-up between you two."

"On the up-and-up?"

"The two of you aren't sleeping together," the older man explained bluntly.

His father was traipsing across territory Paul considered off limits. "Dad, listen, I know you mean well, but I don't think..."

"Paul, I hate to broach the subject, but there've been rumors. It's only natural that there would be. I realize men and women live together without the benefit of marriage all the time. Sadly it's a matter of due course these days."

"Dad, it doesn't bother me what other people think." There would always be those who chose to believe what they wanted to, no matter how innocent the situation.

His father folded his arms over his chest and nodded. "Perhaps not, but how does Leah feel about that?"

Paul was stunned. He hadn't given Leah's reputation a second thought. She was the one who'd suggested moving in with him. He'd assumed, perhaps erroneously, that whatever talk there was about them didn't concern her. Now, imagining anyone criticizing Leah sent the hot blood of fury racing through his veins. He wasn't a man to get angry often, but he was now.

"Who's said something?" he demanded of his father.

"That's not important."

"The hell it isn't...I want to know who the hell..."

"There are a few other, more important matters you should be considering," his father interrupted.

That gave Paul an even greater cause for concern. Had the rumors turned vicious? "Such as?"

"When Leah moved in with you, it's been what? Six, seven weeks now?"

"Something along those lines." Her coming had changed his life. For the first time in nearly a year Paul wasn't suffocating under the burden of emotional pain, suffocating under the strain of nurturing his children alone. Leah had provided much more for him than child care, though. She'd cheered his grief-stricken heart, given him a reason to wake up every morning, showed him the way into the sunlight.

"What about her health insurance?"

"Her health insurance?" Paul exploded. His father had brought Leah's reputation on the line and now he was worried about her health insurance.

"When you mentioned she'd be moving in with you for the next couple of years, I wondered then," his father continued. "From what I understand, the college medical program will only carry her for a few months and then she'll be canceled. In this day and age no one can risk going without insurance."

"I . . . hadn't thought of that." Now that he'd simmered down, Paul felt like a selfish heel. He hadn't even thought to ask Leah about her medical coverage. He'd been so grateful for her help he hadn't stopped to fully consider the cost of her sacrifice.

"What about her other benefits? Will she be losing those, as well?"

"I don't know."

"While we're discussing Leah, let me bring up another subject. Have you had your will altered?" his father pressed.

"My will?"

"Your legal affairs need to be in order, son. If anything were to happen to you now, what would become of the children? With Diane gone, they could be made wards of the state unless some provision for them has been specified in your will."

Paul was stunned by his lack of foresight. "I didn't realize." He expelled his breath slowly and rubbed a weary hand down his face. "I'll make an appointment with James first thing in the morning." Although Christy had broken her engagement with James Wilkens, the attorney remained a good family friend.

"You need to do more than that," his father said emphatically.

"I do?" Paul could only guess at what else he had let slide.

Eric Manning hesitated. It wasn't often Paul saw indecision in his father's face. "You might not like what I'm about to say. You can tell me it's none of my damn business, and you'd be right, but since you asked, I'm going to tell you. I think you should marry Leah. The sooner the better."

"Would you like some iced tea?" Leah asked Paul's mother, struggling to disguise her nervousness.

The sliding glass door was open to the backyard, and she kept her eyes on the twins. Only that morning she'd found the two weeding the garden; unfortunately they'd pulled up the herbs she'd planted with such care.

"No, thank you, my dear." Elizabeth pulled out a kitchen chair and sat down.

Elizabeth hesitated and then lowered her eyes to her hands, folded atop the table as though she, too, were edgy. "I've been meaning to have this talk with you for quite some time. I fear I shouldn't have waited nearly this long."

Leah's heart stopped cold. Paul's mother knew. As hard as she had struggled to hide it, Elizabeth had read the love in her eyes. If she recognized the love, then surely she'd seen the guilt and the confusion.

Leah sank into the chair across from Paul's mother. It was all she could do not to cry out that she'd never meant for Paul to kiss her. Then, composing herself, she sanely realized how utterly foolish that would be.

"Our family is deeply indebted to you, Leah."

"Nonsense."

"For the way you've stepped in and helped Paul and the children. You've made a world of difference in their lives, and ours, too.

"I was terribly worried about Paul after Diane died, you know. For a time I feared he might need some grief therapy, but he gradually worked out his anguish."

"We both have." Learning to deal with her sister's death had been a painful process for Leah, as well.

"The twins are doing so much better," Elizabeth continued. "You were right, they needed their own home and their own toys and familiar friends. These last few weeks have been good ones for Ryan and Ronnie. There's color in their cheeks and they're laughing again. And Kelsey is growing like a weed."

"I found her standing up this morning. That little rascal is going to be walking soon." Leah had a difficult time keeping the pride out of her voice.

Elizabeth beamed. "That's a perfect example of what I mean."

"You give me more credit than you should."

"I doubt it." Elizabeth's smile slowly faded, and her blue eyes grew dark and serious. "I believe you told Paul you'd be willing to stay with him and the children until the boys were in school full-time and Kelsey in preschool?"

Leah nodded. "He won't have the burden of three preschoolers a couple of years down the road. By then he'll be much better able to deal with the situation."

"What do you think will happen to the children after you leave?" Elizabeth asked candidly.

"I'm afraid I don't understand."

"How do you think the twins and Kelsey will react once you move out?" she elaborated.

"That's several years yet, there's no telling how they'll feel."

"I believe there is. The twins have already lost their mother, and we're both well aware of how deeply Diane's death affected them."

Leah said nothing, her heart growing heavy with doubts.

"As for Kelsey...you're the only mother she's ever known."

"Oh, dear," Leah said, and breathed softly. "I never thought...I just didn't realize." She'd been so stupid, so blind. She'd hoped her moving in with Paul would be a solution; instead it was creating more problems. The time would come when she would have to go. She couldn't continue living with Paul indefinitely.

"What should I do?" she asked, thinking aloud, her eyes pleading with Paul's mother. "I can't leave the children now...I love them so much." The very thought produced a sharp pain. A panicky feeling washed over her. She'd been foolish and thoughtless, but it was too late to change matters now.

"I know how deeply you feel about the children."

That was something else Leah had failed to consider—her own feelings in the matter. Her heart was already so tender for these children. She loved them as deeply as if she'd given birth to them herself. It would rip out her soul to walk away from these three little ones.

"There is a solution." Paul's mother's voice came through the haze of regrets that clamored for attention in Leah's mind. "Although you may not fully agree with me."

Leah raised her eyes to Elizabeth's. Her heart was in turmoil. She'd come to live with Paul thinking she would help him and the children. Instead she'd unwittingly created an opportunity to do them irreversible harm.

"Solution?"

"Leah, I fear I've upset you."

"No...no," she countered, reaching for Elizabeth's hands and tightly gripping hold. "You've pointed out some things I should have considered long before now. I can't believe I was so...thoughtless."

Elizabeth nodded and, looking a bit uneasy, asked, "I hope you don't feel I'm prying...but how's your relationship with Paul?"

Leah could feel the hot color swamp her cheeks. "We get along...just fine. We always have. He's wonderful with the children, and I've always liked and respected him." She knew she was talking too fast, but Leah couldn't make herself slow down.

"The two of you are compatible?"

"Oh, yes... we haven't had a single disagreement."
She didn't feel she could count a kiss as a dispute. Perhaps if they were at odds more often, she wouldn't need to battle this growing attraction for him.

"I understand from Paul that you're dating a fellow professor?"

"Some...yes. His name's Bill Mullins, and we have gone out a couple of times in the last few weeks." She didn't mention how she wouldn't be seeing Bill again.

Elizabeth hesitated, and Leah had the impression Paul's mother found this part of the conversation most disconcerting. "Do you hold tender feelings for Bill?"

Leah frowned, not understanding where the older woman was directing the conversation. "Not exactly—we're friends."

Elizabeth seemed relieved at that. Her smile broadened, and she gently squeezed Leah's fingers. "As I said earlier, I think Eric and I may have come across the perfect solution. We talked about it at some length and although we're well aware what happens between you and Paul is none of our concern, we felt we needed to say something."

"Of course."

Elizabeth made a shallow attempt at a smile. "Have you ever thought of marrying Paul?"

Marry Paul?

For some odd reason Leah recalled the night before, when she'd been unable to sleep and had left her room, thinking a gláss of milk would help her insomnia. She hadn't known Paul was up. If she had, she would never have ventured into the hallway. Never have opened her door.

By the time she realized her mistake, it was too late. Although she had plastered herself against the wall in the hallway, willing him to pass her and return to his own room, he had stayed where he was, his eyes searching out hers in the dim light.

Before she could stop herself, Leah had realized they were only inches apart. She'd so desperately wanted his touch that she'd nearly swayed into his arms. When his stubborn chin had caressed the top of her head, she'd wanted his touch so badly she'd had to bite her lip to keep from pleading with him to take her in his arms.

Mere inches had separated them physically. Their noses had brushed; their lips were so close it was a wonder they didn't touch. Leah could only fantasize about what would have happened if they had. Their breaths had entwined.

How they were able to break away from each other without giving in to the hungry demands of their need, Leah didn't know. She hadn't realized it was possible for two people to come so close to making love to each other without even touching.

"Leah?" Elizabeth's voice broke into her thoughts.

"Yes?" Startled, she looked up, surprised to find Paul and his father were in the room.

"I believe we've given these two something to think about," Eric Manning was saying. "I think we should leave them now to talk this out."

Elizabeth stood and Leah did, too, impulsively hugging Paul's mother. She squeezed her eyes closed for a brief moment, while she struggled to find a way to rectify what she'd done. These past few weeks had been some of the happiest of her life. For the first time since childhood, she felt as though she belonged, as though she were needed and loved. But in her ignorance she'd overlooked what should have been obvious. She was confused, unsure. And worse, she didn't know what to do about it. Elizabeth's suggestion wouldn't work. Paul would never want to marry her. Nor should he have to.

Paul and his father exchanged handshakes. Paul escorted his parents to the front door, while Leah set her ice-tea glass in the sink.

When Paul returned to the kitchen, Leah's gaze remained fastened on the kitchen table. Then, seeking, needing his reassurance, her eyes slowly climbed to his.

"Tell me about your health insurance!" Paul asked, sounding angry.

"My health insurance?"

"Yes." It was so rare for Paul to raise his voice that he took her by surprise.

"I could be ruining the children's lives, and you're worried about my health insurance?"

"You've been canceled, haven't you?" he demanded.

Her heart reacted strongly to the cold fury she saw within him. "I don't know...is it important?"

"Yes. And what the hell did you mean you've ruined the children's lives? Sweet heaven, you've been our salvation." He rammed all ten fingers through his hair, pressing his hands against his head. "I'm the one who's been so damn selfish." He walked away from her and then pivoted sharply. "Why the hell didn't you say something?"

"About my health insurance? Trust me, Paul, there were other more important matters I was dealing with."

"Like planting a garden?"

"Yes, like planting a garden." She didn't understand his anger. It was so unlike him. From what little she could tell, the anger wasn't directed at her, but himself. She couldn't understand that, either.

She turned away from him, fighting tears. "If it'll make you happy, I'll see to it first thing in the morning. Why are you acting like this?"

"My father pointed out a few home truths I should have thought of myself. I can't believe I've been so obtuse. I should never have allowed you to move in with me."

Leah thought she was going to be physically sick. Paul was going to send her away. For all the reasons his mother had mentioned.

"No." Her cry came straight from her heart. "I won't let you do it."

"Do what?"

"Make me leave. I'll fight you. I'll even fight your parents, but I won't let you send me away from the twins and Kelsey." *And from you,* she added silently.

"Send you away?" Paul repeated, aghast. "I should never have let you come, but now that you're here, I couldn't make you go...." He hesitated and went still and pale. "Unless that was what you wanted."

Tears of release and relief filled her eyes. She brushed them aside, not wanting Paul to know how badly she'd needed his assurance.

"Do you want to leave, Leah?"

She glared at him, her eyes dewy and defiant. "No...I just got done telling you as much."

He sighed and took one step toward her, then stopped, his look intense. "Did my mother offer the same solution to you as my dad did me?"

Leah watched him closely, hoping to read his reaction. "She . . . thought we should marry."

"And?"

"And . . . I haven't had time to mull it over, but it seems . . . above and beyond the call of duty for you to have to marry me."

Paul's eyes narrowed as he studied her. Apparently he didn't understand.

"I already explained I'm not the marrying kind."

"I never have understood that attitude. You're a warm, gracious, generous woman. What makes you think you're so unmarriageable?"

Leah laughed nervously. She'd never garnered much attention from the opposite sex, not even when she was younger and prettier. She was much too bookish for most men. Too intelligent. Falling in love had escaped her in her twenties, and by the time she was thirty, she'd given up hope of finding a husband.

"I'm serious," Paul demanded, sounding angry again.

Leah hesitated. Her heart was racing with hope. For the first time in her life she had a chance at happiness, a promise of something more than she'd ever dared dream. A family. Home. Love. That she was stealing it from her sister was of little consequence. Diane had come to her in the dream. Diane had sent her to Paul and the children.

"Are . . . are you saying you'd be willing to marry me?"

Paul buried his hands in his pants pockets. "Yes, if it wasn't so unfair to you."

"Unfair?"

"Leah, for the love of heaven, look around you. I'm raising three motherless children. I'll be paying two more years on Diane's hospital bills and..."

"I know all that."

"I don't have anything to offer you."

Only a wealth beyond her wildest dreams—a wealth that had nothing to do with material items. He was offering her more love than she'd ever thought to find in ten lifetimes. An abundant harvest of flowers in a life that nourished cacti.

"What about children I love? A home and a family."

Paul's gaze connected with hers. He looked uncertain, as if he wasn't sure he should be asking. "That would be enough for you?"

Leah nodded.

His voice was gruff with emotion when he next spoke. "Will you marry me, Leah, for all our sakes?"

In a heartbeat. "Yes," she whispered, "I'll marry you, Paul."

Chapter Seven

"We're mature adults," Leah said, conscious of sounding anything but. "We both realize this isn't a love match."

"We're going into this with our eyes wide open," Paul elaborated.

"Exactly." The relief she felt knowing she wouldn't be forced to leave the children was so great that Leah relaxed in the kitchen chair, holding her head up with her hands. She brushed the loose strands of hair from her forehead and smiled weakly up at Paul.

"There is love involved, though," Paul said pointedly, studying her.

She'd never been more aware of a man's look. Engrossed. Absorbed. The very eyes she considered so beautiful she made a point of avoiding. Since the night they'd kissed, she had noticed that Paul looked at her differently. Once again she wished she were more experienced in relationships, for she couldn't say what it was about Paul's look that wasn't the same. Leah felt at a loss to explain it even to herself. She gave a deep, reflective sigh and glanced up to notice Paul's gaze hadn't wavered. He was waiting for her to embellish his statement.

"Naturally there's love involved," she said, rushing the words together, speaking too quickly. "We both love the children," she added, hating the breathless quality that bled into her words.

Paul scooted out a chair and sat across from her. "The children are an important factor, but there's far more involved here than three small children. I want to know what you feel for me."

Leah had come to know a directness about Paul that she loved...and hated. Her own mind was far more analytical, often meandering and subtle. To her, everything needed to be taken into account, organized in a logical manner and then carefully reviewed. It was the way she lived her life.

Paul, on the other hand, had neither the time nor the patience to mull over issues. He wrote on a deadline, straight off the top of his head. To him, it shouldn't take more than five minutes to analyze a situation.

Defining feelings seemed to come much easier for him, too. Leah had always found that difficult, as well.

"Leah?" Paul prodded when she didn't answer right away.

"I don't know what I feel for you." It was an honest answer...as honest as she dared. She was afraid to love him, and even more frightened that she already did. She was afraid to admit how much she wanted him, even to herself. He made her experience a myriad of emotions, physical desires, she didn't know she was capable of feeling.

"What do you expect from this marriage?" Paul asked her next.

"I...don't know that, either. I haven't had time to think about it." The thought struck her, one she should have considered much earlier. "What exactly...do you expect?"

"A wife."

He left it at that, left it for her imagination to fill in the blanks. "I see."

"Do you, Leah? After we're married, I'll want you to move into my bedroom with me, to share my life and my bed." He hesitated as though he expected an argument. "I realize you don't love me now, but I'm hoping you will in time. Do you have a problem with that?"

Talking so openly had always made Leah uneasy. She lowered her gaze. "No...but do you honestly believe we can make a marriage work?"

"Of course, otherwise I would never agree to it, and neither would you."

"I've been so obtuse," she said, thinking of her conversation with his mother. "I can't believe I was so thoughtless...so callous not to consider what would become of the children after I moved out."

"I wasn't thinking clearly myself."

"It's so unlike me."

"I know. Me too."

"Why did it take your parents so long to say something?" The concerns Elizabeth raised were valid ones and should have been voiced much sooner, Leah thought.

"I asked my dad the same thing," Paul told her. "He claimed it wasn't until recently that he thought of these matters himself."

"I just wish they'd said something sooner."

"I do, too," Paul agreed.

Paul glanced at his watch, checking the time. He only had an hour for his lunch break and Leah was already five minutes late. He knew something must have detained her since she was as punctual as she was honest.

Pacing the hallway outside the licensing office in the King County Courthouse, he mulled over the changes of the past couple of days. For the first time in nearly a week, he'd slept soundly. The erotic fantasies involving Leah that had hounded him for several restless nights had eased. When he went to bed, he closed his eyes half-fearing she'd stroll into his mind, bold as can be. A vision of her had made nightly appearances since he'd kissed her. She would smile at him, slow and sweet, and then his imagination would take over, tormenting him for hours on end.

But it hadn't happened since Leah had agreed to marry him. Perhaps it was because he knew that it was only a matter of time before he made love to her. He'd made certain the night of his parents' visit that Leah understood that theirs would be a real marriage. He didn't want any last-minute surprises.

There'd been a time, not all that distant, when he would have pleaded with God to help him, pleaded with Diane to forgive him and wallowed in a swim-

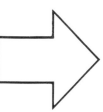

NO COST! NO OBLIGATION TO BUY!
NO PURCHASE NECESSARY!

PLAY "LUCKY 7"
AND GET AS MANY AS SIX FREE GIFTS...

HOW TO PLAY:

1. With a coin, carefully scratch off the silver box at the right. This makes you eligible to receive two or more free books, and possibly other gifts, depending on what is revealed beneath the scratch-off area.

2. You'll receive brand-new Silhouette Special Edition® novels. When you return this card, we'll send you the books and gifts you qualify for *absolutely free!*

3. If we don't hear from you, every month, we'll send you 6 additional novels to read and enjoy. You can return them and owe nothing but if you decide to keep them, you'll pay only $2.96* per book, a saving of 43¢ each off the cover price plus only 69¢ delivery for the entire shipment!

4. When you join the Silhouette Reader Service™, you'll get our subscribers'-only newsletter, as well as additional free gifts from time to time just for being a subscriber.

5. You must be completely satisfied. You may cancel at any time simply by sending us a note or a shipping statement marked "cancel" or by returning any shipment to us at our cost.

*Terms and prices subject to change without notice. Canadian residents add applicable federal and provincial taxes.   © 1990 HARLEQUIN ENTERPRISES LIMITED

This lovely heart-shaped box is richly detailed with cut-glass decorations, perfect for holding a precious memento or keepsake—and it's yours absolutely free when you accept our no-risk offer.

PLAY "LUCKY 7"

**Just scratch off the silver box with a coin.
Then check below to see which gifts you get.**

YES! I have scratched off the silver box. Please send me all the gifts for which I qualify. I understand I am under no obligation to purchase any books, as explained on the opposite page.

335 CIS AEQ3
(C-SIL-SE-06/92)

NAME

ADDRESS   APT

CITY   PROVINCE   POSTAL CODE

| 7 | 7 | 7 | WORTH FOUR FREE BOOKS, FREE HEART-SHAPED GLASS BOX AND MYSTERY BONUS |

| 🍒 | 🍒 | 🍒 | WORTH FOUR FREE BOOKS AND MYSTERY BONUS |

| ● | ● | ● | WORTH THREE FREE BOOKS |

| 🔔 | 🔔 | 🍒 | WORTH TWO FREE BOOKS |

SILHOUETTE ''NO RISK'' GUARANTEE

- You're not required to buy a single book—ever!
- You must be completely satisfied or you may cancel at any time simply by sending us a note or a shipping statement marked ''cancel'' or returning any shipment to us at our cost. Either way, you will receive no more books; you'll have no obligation to buy.
- The free books and gifts you receive from this ''Lucky 7'' offer remain yours to keep no matter what you decide.

Business Reply Mail

No Postage Stamp Necessary if Mailed in Canada

Postage will be paid by

SILHOUETTE READER SERVICE
PO BOX 609
FORT ERIE, ONT.
L2A 9Z9

ming pool of guilt for just thinking of making love to his sister-in-law. He felt an acceptance now, an inevitability.

He needed Leah. Not for the physical release her body would yield him, although that was part of it. He needed her the way a man needs substance. Fresh air. Water. Food. She was a part of his life now. An important part. Just as she was vital to his children, Leah was vital to him. His world revolved around her. He woke in the morning and his first thoughts were of her. Several times during the workday he found himself looking at his watch and calculating how long it would be before he could return home. He wasn't sure when all this had started to happen or even if it was a good thing. All he knew was that it was going on.

Did he love Leah?

Paul didn't know. Certainly what he felt for her was unlike his love for Diane. In the months since her death, Paul realized he could be more objective about his marriage to Leah's younger sister. He loved Diane all through his soul. He had never experienced grief on a deeper level than when he'd lost her. She was unselfish and gentle, and in his heart he knew she wouldn't have wanted him to live alone. In his own way he believed Diane would have approved of him marrying Leah. Of Leah raising her children.

To Paul's way of thinking, if he was to marry a second time, Leah was the perfect choice. For the obvious reasons, yes, but the not so obvious ones, too.

In marrying Leah, he'd still be able to hold on to Diane, remain emotionally faithful to her. The two sisters would forever be linked in his mind. Leah shared his love for Diane, and that alone averted a storehouse of resentments and potential problems in a second marriage. Leah understood and appreciated his love for her sister. She wouldn't make unreasonable demands on him in an effort to force Diane out of his life.

Leah's question about why it took so long for his parents to bring up the issues that concerned them came to Paul's mind. He wondered the same thing himself. He wasn't completely satisfied by his father's answer. Less than a month ago, if anyone had recommended he remarry, Paul would have resisted the suggestion, no matter who the proposed partner was. Even Leah. He hadn't been ready, emotionally or any other way. His father's timing in broaching the subject had been impeccable.

"Paul." Leah sighed his name as she hurried down the wide courthouse corridor, walking at a clipped pace. "I'm so sorry I'm late."

She looked nice, Paul noted. Her hair was combed stylishly and she wore a flowered dress, belted at the middle in a simple but flattering design.

"I hope I haven't kept you waiting long," she said, sounding winded.

"No more than five minutes."

"The baby-sitter was late, and then I couldn't find a parking place and . . ."

"You're here now and that's all that matters."

She placed her hand over her heart as though to stop its pounding, and Paul resisted the urge to put his arm around her and comfort her. He found himself looking for excuses to touch her, but thus far had resisted. His fear was that once he did, he wouldn't be able to stop. A touch would lead to a kiss and a kiss would lead to . . . God only knew what.

"We can apply for the marriage license over here," he said, directing her through the double doors that led to the office.

She nodded, then hesitated before entering the doorway. "You're sure you want to go through with this?" she whispered without looking at him.

If either of them was going to entertain second thoughts, the time was now. Yet Paul didn't hesitate. He knew what he wanted; he wanted Leah. "Positive. What about you?"

Her smile was gentle, sweet. "I'm here, aren't I?"

Applying for the marriage license took a quick five minutes. Paul was pleased Leah had opted to leave the children with a sitter. For the first time since she'd moved in with him, he had uninterrupted time alone with her.

"How about lunch?"

His invitation seemed to surprise and please her. "I'd like that."

There was a popular bookstore off First Avenue with a small restaurant in the basement. Paul ate there often and enjoyed the library feel of the place. It wasn't fancy; it wasn't even close to fancy. Certainly not the type of restaurant a man took a woman he wanted to impress. But it was the perfect place for them. A restaurant Paul knew Leah would love.

They stood in line to place their order, then found a table in the back of the room, next to an old brick wall decorated with books and several pieces by local artists.

"This is perfect," Leah said, glancing around, seeming to soak in the ambience.

"I thought you'd appreciate it."

She smiled shyly. "I have some exciting news."

"Oh?"

"Kelsey took her first step this morning."

Leah looked as proud and pleased as if his daughter had flown to the moon and back by her own power. "It was bound to happen any day now."

"The boys were as excited as I was."

"I remember when Ryan and Ronnie were that age."

A waitress delivered their order of bubbling chicken pot pies and hot coffee.

Leah reached for her fork. "Who walked first, Ryan or Ronnie?"

"Ryan. He wanted his blankie, and since I was holding it out to him, the most expedient way to collect it was to take a few staggering steps in my direction. As I recall, Ronnie refused to allow his brother to outdo him and walked almost immediately afterward."

"It's difficult to remember the boys at a year old," Leah said with a happy sigh.

Paul nodded, then a thought came to him. "Leah, let's not talk about the children."

Her gaze shot up, and her eyes, which were a cross between green and blue from the flowered dress she wore, revealed her bewilderment. "Why not?"

"Because soon we're going to be married."

"You ... want to discuss that?" She sounded worried.

"No. In time the children will be gone. At some point in the future there'll only be the two of us. We both love the children, that's a given. We've agreed to marry, each for our own reasons, but in the end it'll boil down to the two of us. We're going to need to build a relationship.''

''A relationship,'' she repeated the words as though they were uncomfortable on her tongue.

''You might be more at ease if we call it a friendship.''

Leah nodded. ''You're right, of course . . . it's just that I'm not very good at this sort of thing. You'll probably need to help me.''

After all that Leah had given to him of herself, of her life, that he would be able to assist her in some small way gladdened Paul's heart. If he'd been forced to find fault with Leah, it would be her stubborn self-reliance. He understood and recognized it because he was fiercely independent himself. As the oldest of five children, he had learned early in life that he needed to be.

''What shall we talk about?'' Leah asked softly.

''Anything we like.''

An earsplitting silence followed. They had lived together for nearly two months. They had agreed to marry. They planned to spend the rest of their natural lives together. Yet, when Paul took the children out of the conversation, they had nothing to say.

''Oh dear,'' Leah said, her eyes filled with alarm. She set the fork next to her chicken pot pie. ''This is more difficult than I realized.''

''Do you want to tell me about your garden, Mary Contrary?''

Her eyes brightened briefly, but after a moment or two the enthusiasm quickly drained. ''What's there to tell you? It's growing nicely.''

''My parents keep a garden,'' Paul volunteered.

"Did they ever grow herbs?"

"Not to my knowledge."

"What about zucchini?"

"Enough to feed the entire state of Texas," Paul said, remembering that his dad routinely dropped off huge amounts of the vegetable. Paul hadn't the heart to tell him he'd rather eat gravel than the zucchini. At least Diane had found a recipe—zucchini-chocolate cake—that made it tolerable to him.

Their conversation got off to a slow start, but by the end of the hour, Paul felt they had made good headway.

When they'd finished with their lunch, Paul walked Leah back to where she had parked the car. Although he was already late getting back to the office, he found himself reluctant to leave her. He'd be home in a matter of hours, but he wanted to hold on to this time alone with her. Learn more about her, the woman he was about to marry.

Leah didn't seem eager to leave, either. She held her car keys in her hands, glancing down at them periodically.

It came to Paul then how much he would have liked to kiss her. But it wasn't the type of thing he was comfortable doing on a busy Seattle street. He knew any public display of affection would only embarrass Leah. Diane would have spontaneously tossed her arms around his neck and kissed him silly regardless of where they were or who was watching.

But it wasn't Diane he was marrying; it was Leah.

A fact Paul had best remember.

* * *

Leah woke the morning of her wedding day to bright sunshine. Paul had contacted a minister friend who'd agreed to perform a private ceremony. They arranged everything quickly, quietly. They hadn't said anything to Paul's family. Leah wasn't sure Paul intended on saying anything until afterward, which suited her fine. Having his mother hover over her would have made Leah more nervous than she already was.

She didn't doubt that she was doing the right thing, marrying Paul, but she wasn't one to stand on ceremony. His family would have insisted on making something more out of it than Leah wanted.

Leah had purchased a white linen suit for the occasion. Normally she didn't wear a hat, but she had found one she rather liked and it looked good on her. The saleslady had been very helpful, and Leah was grateful for the added touch of style.

Diane had always gone with her when she needed to buy something for a special occasion. How ironic it was that Leah had never yearned for her sister's opinion more than she did in trying to choose what to wear when she married Paul.

The ceremony itself took only a matter of minutes. Filling out the marriage license had been more involved than the wedding itself. They had both opted for plain gold bands and Paul's eyes had held hers when he'd slipped the ring on her finger. His eyes were warm and reassuring. Leah hoped hers were the same when her turn came.

Afterwards Paul kissed her briefly. Although his mouth had barely grazed hers, a riot of sensation came rushing at Leah. She trembled in his arms and prayed he didn't guess how strong her sensual response was to him.

When they left the church office, Paul suggested they stop off and visit his parents.

"Sure," Leah agreed. The children were with them and would need to go down for their afternoon naps soon, but there was time for a brief visit.

Elizabeth looked mildly surprised when she opened her front door. "Paul, Leah," she greeted warmly, holding open the screen door. "This is a pleasant surprise. Come in, please." She took Kelsey out of Paul's arms and set her granddaughter on the carpet. "I understand she's walking now."

"Just watch. This kid's headed for the Olympics at the rate she's going," Paul said proudly.

"Paul." His father strolled into the living room, looking pleased at their unexpected arrival. "Sit down, sit down."

Leah opted for the sectional, and Paul sat next to her. The boys hurried into the kitchen and stood in front of the counter, waiting for their grandmother to give them a cookie out of the cookie jar.

Elizabeth complied with a smile, then joined the adults in the living room. If Paul's parents noticed that he and Leah were overly dressed for an early Saturday afternoon, neither commented.

Paul reached for Leah's hand, gently squeezed her fingers with his own, then looked to his parents. "Leah and I stopped off to tell you we've taken your advice. We were married a little more than an hour ago."

"Married," his mother cried as though she'd never heard the word before.

"Married," his father boomed, vaulting to his feet.

Perplexed, Leah turned to look at her husband. Perhaps they'd misunderstood. Perhaps the two of them marrying wasn't what his parents had urged. But Leah had been so sure it was. In the time since the elder Mannings' visit, she had realized the purpose of their talks—one with Paul, the other with her—was to bring them each separately to the point where they could see how much sense it made for the two of them to marry.

Elizabeth started to weep softly.

"Mom?" Paul made no effort to disguise his confusion. "Good grief, I'd think you'd be happy."

"I am."

"Then why the tears?"

"Because you're just like Taylor and Christy."

"Don't forget Rich," Eric snapped, sounded equally distressed.

"What do the girls have to do with Leah and me?"

"First Taylor married Russ in Reno. She didn't have a single family member there. Not one. Your father and I could have been there in less than two hours by plane. Out of the blue she marries a cowboy she's known less than three months."

"Then Christy married Cody," Eric went on, sounding equally disturbed. "In Idaho, no less. She flies off to a neighboring state to get married for fear her family might find out about it."

"If you'll recall," Paul noted, "she was still engaged to James at the time."

"She didn't even let Taylor in on what she was doing until much later." Elizabeth reached for a tissue and loudly blew her nose. "If it wasn't bad enough that your sisters married without family being there, Rich

opted to have an ordinary judge marry him and Jamie."

"That was because they were planning their divorce
shortly afterward," Paul said, defending his brother's
actions.

"He was planning a divorce?" Confused, Leah
whispered the question in Paul's ear.

"I'll tell you about it later," he promised.

Vaguely Leah remembered Diane telling her the details of Rich's marriage to Jamie Warren. As she recalled, the couple had gotten married for the express
purpose of bearing a child. She seemed to remember
Diane explaining the two had originally intended Jamie be artificially inseminated, but by the time Rich's
wife became pregnant, there hadn't been anything ar-
tificial about it.

"You mean you're upset because we didn't invite you
to the ceremony?" Paul asked.

His parents shared an incredulous look.

"Yes." His father's loud voice boomed through the
house. "Good grief, what is it about you children?
Don't you have an inkling of how badly your mother
and I want to attend a wedding in this family? We have
five children, four of them married, and we've yet to
be invited to a single child's wedding."

"Dad, Mom, I'm sorry," Paul said, sounding genuinely contrite.

Leah felt terrible. She should have said something to
encourage Paul to mention their decision to his family. Her thoughts had been selfish. She was afraid
Elizabeth would have made a fuss, something Leah had
wished to avoid.

"I apologize, too," Leah said meekly.

"The deed's done now," Eric said, tight-lipped, then made an effort to relax and let go of his disappointment. "There's no need to cry over spilled milk."

"I promise if I ever get married again, I'll be sure you and Mom are there for the ceremony."

Although she knew Paul was joking, Leah felt a small twinge of anxiety and possessiveness.

"Jason's our last hope for a large family wedding," Elizabeth said, dabbing her eyes with the tissue.

"Jason," Paul repeated, barely holding back a laugh. "I hate to disappoint you, but I can't see Jason ever marrying. He's too set in his ways."

"God's going to find that son of mine a wife," Elizabeth said, her voice raised righteously. "I can't believe the good Lord would give me five beautiful children and then cheat me out of the pleasure of putting on a wedding."

"I'm sure everything will work out for the best," Paul assured his parents.

The boys started squabbling, and Leah knew it was because they were tired and hadn't had their lunch. Kelsey was about to fall asleep, as well.

"We should be going," Leah said, looking to Paul. "I feel so badly we disappointed you," she added to the Mannings. "I do hope you'll forgive us for being so thoughtless." She stood, reaching for Kelsey. The little girl pressed her head against Leah's shoulder and yawned sleepily.

"Where are you two headed for your honeymoon?" Eric asked.

Paul and Leah exchanged shocked glances. "We hadn't actually planned a honeymoon."

"I certainly hope you intend to get away for the night at least."

Once again Paul cast an apologetic look to Leah. "Actually I . . . we hadn't discussed it."

"That's no excuse," Elizabeth said, a feisty look in her eye. "You're to leave the children with your father and me and the two of you are to take the rest of the day and night to yourselves."

Leah wanted to object, but was immediately cut off. "But . . ."

"There's no buts about it. You're family now, although I've always considered you part of our family anyway. Now it's official. And I won't allow this cantankerous son of mine to cheat his bride."

"What about the children's things?"

"You can drop them off later. I'll feed them lunch and put them down for a nap and everything will be just fine, won't it, boys?"

Spending time with their grandparents had always been a special treat, and the twins were eager for the opportunity.

"You're sure this isn't too much trouble?" Leah whispered. Since Kelsey was already asleep, Leah carried her into the crib that was set up in the Mannings' spare bedroom.

"No problem whatsoever," Elizabeth insisted. "You and Paul go and have a nice uninterrupted day. I'll drop the children off after church in the morning."

"This is really very thoughtful of you."

"Nonsense. It's the least Eric and I can do." Paul's mother hugged her briefly. "I'm so pleased for you and Paul. I couldn't imagine him finding a better wife."

Leah had no illusions about her marriage. As she and Paul had discussed earlier, theirs wasn't a love match. Although Paul had made certain she understood she'd be sharing his bed, for all intents and purposes it was a marriage of convenience.

It was convenient for him. Convenient for the children. Convenient for her.

"Thank you again," Leah said when Paul's mother escorted her to the front door.

Paul helped her into the car. The twins and their grandparents stood on the front lawn and waved as Paul started the car and they drove away.

Her husband was strangely quiet for several minutes. Without the children as a buffer Leah felt awkward and ill at ease.

"I'm sorry, Leah," he said after several tense minutes.

"For what?"

"For cheating you."

"Cheating me? I don't understand." She didn't feel the least bit slighted. Her wedding was exactly the way she had wanted it. Intimate, with only the children present.

"Mom and Dad were right. I should have planned a honeymoon trip for us. It was extremely inconsiderate of me."

"I don't want a trip."

"Perhaps not, but you deserve one. You deserve a whole lot more than I'm giving you." He sounded angry, but his disappointment was in himself and not directed at her.

"Stop right this minute, Paul Manning."

"Stop? We're on the freeway."

"I was speaking figuratively."

"Oh."

"It's not your job to read my mind. If I want something, I'll ask for it. All right?"

"All right."

A few minutes passed. "What about our wedding night?"

"What about it?" Leah grew uneasy discussing the subject.

"Do you want to go to a hotel?"

"No." Her response was immediate. A hotel would only make her more nervous than she was already.

"Why not?"

"Well...because...you might feel pressured to make love to me."

"Feel pressured?" She thought she detected a note of humor in his tone.

"I...I think our marriage would be better served if we delayed the physical aspect of our...relationship, don't you? I mean...what I'm trying to say is that...well, we hardly have anything to talk about without the children. Remember what it was like at lunch the other day? It makes perfect sense to me that we should develop a solid friendship before we...you know."

"The term is make love," Paul returned impatiently.

"Right...before we make love." It was difficult for her to speak so openly, but she made the effort because too much was at stake. Their whole lives stretched before them. It seemed to her there was plenty of time for them to become comfortable with one another without rushing into the physical aspects of the marriage.

"You agree, don't you?" she asked timidly.

Paul didn't answer right away. "We'll sleep together in the same bed."

She noted he left no room for question. "If you want."

"I most certainly do."

"I'm agreeable to that." Leah found herself wishing they had discussed this earlier.

"What about tonight?" he demanded. "If you don't want to go to a hotel, exactly how do you suggest we spend the night?"

Leah hesitated. "Would you mind very much if we just stayed home?"

Chapter Eight

"**Y**ou want to stay home." Paul was certain he hadn't heard her right. Not only had she opted to skip a honeymoon, but she also wanted to entirely do away with their wedding night. If that was what she really wished, then fine, he could accept that. He didn't like it, but he could accept it. But staying home, that was another matter entirely.

"There's so much to do."

"Like what?"

She hesitated only slightly, but enough for Paul to notice. "I...thought I'd use this afternoon to move my things into your bedroom."

"Good idea. But what about tonight?"

"Tonight?" she echoed, her voice slightly elevated with what sounded like nervousness.

"We should do something special."

"I thought...we'd already decided...not to, you know...haven't we? We'd agreed to hold off on the..."

"I was thinking more along the lines of going out to dinner."

"Oh."

The silence between them was filled with high-octane tension.

"You don't need to worry, Leah, I'm not going to ravish your body." Paul didn't know how this marriage was going to survive with Leah's current attitude. He'd only kissed her the two times. The first had been one of the most beautiful, sensual experiences of his life. The second had been shortly after the wedding ceremony, and although it had been little more than a brushing of lips, Paul had felt the hot current of need surge between them. She could deny it if she chose, but he wasn't willing to tiptoe around it. Their bodies were starved for one another, at near fever pitch.

Yet Leah seemed determined to place them under this self-imposed sexual abstinence. It made no sense, and frankly it was frustrating the hell out of Paul.

When his parents had offered to take the children, Paul had entertained thoughts of bringing Leah home, carrying her over the threshold and directly into his bedroom. He'd envisioned an afternoon of introducing her to the physical delights of marriage. After dinner he'd introduce her all over again.

Paul pulled into the driveway, turned off the engine and sat for a few moments in an effort to collect his thoughts.

"We can go out to dinner, if you like," she offered weakly.

He nodded. Starting off their marriage with an argument wasn't a healthy sign, in light of the fact that they'd hardly spoken crossly to each other before. Apparently they were saving all their arguing for the honeymoon period.

Paul went around to help her out of the car, and Leah smiled up at him, her eyes wide and imploring. Try as he might, he couldn't resist her and he returned the gesture, however weak.

So she wanted to build a solid relationship before they decided to make love. He could understand that. He didn't like admitting it, but the idea made sense. He could live with it.

He prayed he could live with it.

Once inside the house, they moved into their separate bedrooms and changed clothes. As Paul pulled the tie loose from his neck, he wondered just how long Leah intended on them holding off. He walked over to the closet and stood, staring blankly at the row of hanging clothes, his mind soaking up the question.

Would she make him wait a week? He could endure a week.

What about a month? Out of the question.

He removed his shirt, then, sitting on the end of the bed, he untied his shoe and slipped it off his foot.

He didn't realize he'd been there so long mulling over the situation until he heard Leah outside the bedroom.

"Paul?"

"Yes."

"I'm ready to bring in some of my things."

"Just a minute." He finished changing in record time, then opened the door. She stood on the other side in a blouse and faded jeans, holding a load of clothes in her arms. Paul took them from her and carried them to the bed.

"I was thinking I could move my things, and you could take a change of clothes for the children over to your parents' place."

"Sure," he said amicably enough. He wasn't eager to leave her, but it might be for the best. He'd put the time to good use, ponder over what he was going to do about this nonmarriage-marriage.

"Do you want some lunch before you go? You must be starving... you didn't have anything to eat this morning, did you? I know I didn't."

"No, thanks." He shoved his car keys into his jeans pocket.

"But aren't you hungry?"

His eyes found hers. "Yes, Leah, I'm hungry," he informed her heatedly. "I'm starving to death."

His exit made for excellent drama, Paul realized, but it didn't do anything to improve his mood.

They were married, damn it. He had the legal document to confirm it, and he'd never wanted a woman more. That he couldn't have her, couldn't taste her kiss, couldn't sink his body into hers only fueled his anger... and his hunger. She was his, but he couldn't claim her.

Paul hadn't come to any conclusions by the time he returned to the house. He must have left his poor parents wondering. He'd driven into their driveway, gotten out of the car, walked to the door, waited until his mother answered, handed her the clothes Leah had packed for the kids and a fresh stack of diapers for Kelsey, turned around and left.

He thought he might have heard his mother call after him, but if that was the case, he'd ignored her. He also thought he might have heard his father chuckling, telling Paul's mother she should recognize a man in a hurry when she saw one.

Paul was in a hurry, all right, but he didn't have anywhere to go.

By the time he returned to the house, Leah had emptied her bedroom and transported her things into his. A hell of a lot of good sleeping in the same bed was going to do them. Apparently Leah planned to torture him to death.

"I . . . fixed you some lunch."

"Thanks." He made the effort to smile his appreciation as he walked into the kitchen.

She followed but kept several feet of protective distance between them. What did she think, he was going to attack her? The hell if Paul knew.

"You're angry with me, aren't you?" she asked, folding her hands in front of her.

"No."

"You are. I can tell . . . I'm not good at these things. Di— My sister was always so much better at dealing with feelings than I was . . . dealing with men, too. You regret marrying me already and . . ."

She sounded close to tears. Whatever anger or frustration Paul was experiencing died a sudden death. He walked over to her and took her into his arms, wanting to ease her distress.

"I'm sorry," he breathed into her hair, loving the feel of her in his arms. With his index finger he brushed a strand of hair from her face.

"I feel like a total failure as a wife and we haven't even been married twenty-four hours." He heard the tears in her voice and he felt like the biggest heel who ever lived. He had behaved like a little boy who'd had his candy taken away from him. If anyone was to blame, it was him.

"I'm the one who should be sorry," he whispered.

"You?" She lifted her head and looked up at him. "But why?"

"Because I've acted like a major jerk."

"You're disappointed because I wanted to wait before we...made love?"

He nodded.

"I didn't think you'd want me."

"Not want you?"

She lowered her eyes and went completely still. The only movement she made was the rise and fall of her chest as she gently breathed. "I'm not pretty."

"Leah, for the love of heaven, you're so damn beautiful you take my breath away."

"Please, don't lie to me. I know my assets and my weaknesses and..."

Paul reacted to instinct, framing her face in his hands, his eyes searching out hers. Whatever else she'd intended to say died as his mouth claimed hers. He'd apparently caught her off guard—what the hell, his need came as a shock even to himself. Leah fastened her hands against his chest, and after a moment of surprise passed, she parted her lips to him.

Paul groaned. He hurt. He ached. He was instantly hard, a fact he cursed, then prized as he anchored his hands at her hips and dragged her against him.

Leah groaned, too, and he took her mouth again, this time long and slow instead of hungry and demanding. Paul found himself drowning in hot, encompassing sensation. He had to touch her, had to know for himself the silken feel of her. Gently, so not to frighten her, his fingertips grazed her nipple as his hand adjusted to the shape and feel of her breast in his palm.

Leah groaned anew.

"Am I hurting you?"

"No."

"Frightening you?"

"Yes."

He started to move his hand away.

"No," she pleaded, gripping hold of his wrist. "What frightens me are the wonderful things you make me feel."

He braced his feet farther apart. "Do you feel what you do to me?"

Her eyes were closed, her lips dewy and parted as she slowly nodded.

Paul kissed her again, easing his tongue forward. Leah's tongue shyly met his, and they touched, rubbed, stroked, then curled around each other's. Again and again he kissed her. Softly. Quickly. Teasingly. Slowly.

It was either stop completely or explode right then and there. His control was quickly slipping out of his grasp. Where he found the strength, Paul didn't know, but he pulled his mouth from hers and opened his eyes.

Leah's own eyes fluttered open with surprise and disappointment. They were brown-green, and hazy with passion. "Paul?"

"Hmm . . ."

"I..."

"You're beautiful," he reiterated.

She stiffened, but Paul continued to hold her, refusing to release her. "I love the color of your eyes. They intrigue me, the way they change. So many shades of color, of meaning... like a window to your soul."

She blushed, but Paul hadn't even begun to tell her all the things he found exquisitely special about her. "You have no idea how beautiful your hair looks when the sunshine plays on it." His heart wanted to tell her about the afternoon he'd found her working in the backyard with the children around her, but he couldn't find the words.

"I love your mouth."

To prove it he kissed her, leisurely, thoroughly.

"Paul," she sighed.

"But most of all," he said breathlessly, "I love your laugh."

"Oh, Paul."

"So don't you dare tell me you're not beautiful again."

"You make me want to cry."

Paul smiled. "You've helped dry my tears, Leah. I want you so much."

"You do?"

Once again he settled his hands on either side of her waist and dragged her against his arousal. "Feel how hard I am? How could you think I wouldn't desire you? I want you very much." He nestled her softness against him one more time in a way she couldn't ignore.

"Your argument is well-taken," she said, smiling softly.

He kissed her and slid his tongue deep into her mouth, prowling at will. He found breaking away almost impossible, so he nibbled at her lips, softly, repeatedly, until she was seeking out his kiss, needing him.

"Are you sure you want to wait?" Paul whispered.

"Ah . . . I'm not sure of anything at the moment."

"Let me taste you, Leah," he pleaded. His fingers were busy unfastening the buttons of her blouse. "Just one taste."

"Paul . . . I don't . . . I've never."

"Then it's time."

How or when they made it from the kitchen to the bedroom, Paul didn't know. He pressed her against the mattress and bent over her. Reverently he touched her, fearing the power of his need would frighten her, and that was the last thing he wanted. Taking his time, his hands trembling as he shifted his position, kneeling above her, he spread open her blouse. Her bra hooked in the back, and he deftly probed behind her, releasing the clasp. With a little help from her, he removed the shirt and bra.

He paused, looking down on her and marveling at the perfection he found. "Your breasts are beautiful, too. Plump and generous."

"Paul . . ."

He held them cupped in his palms. Gently he rubbed the pad of his thumb over the nipples, which peaked and pouted.

The passion she stirred in him was almost more than he could bear. Slowly, delaying the pleasure, Paul lowered his face to her bounty and gently closed his mouth over the tip of her right breast. Leah trembled as his lips fastened over her nipple. His nimble tongue circled the bud gently, until he was assured she was comfortable with his presence, then he gradually increased the pressure until he was taking full suckle.

Leah squirmed beneath him, but Paul continued his feast, dividing his attention between her breasts. Leah made strangled sounds, but Paul continued until he was sure he'd pleasured her adequately.

Leah was panting, her hands gripping hold of the bedspread, as though she needed something to moor her to the bed.

"Was that painful for you, Leah?"

"No."

"Pleasurable?"

She nodded, her eyes closed.

Eager now, pleased with the progress they'd made, Paul shucked off his shirt. He tossed it aside, then gradually lowered himself over her until they were chest to breast. Her softness seemed to close in around him.

"Leah." He breathed her name, finding no other words to describe the pleasure she gave him.

He felt her heart pounding, steady and strong against him. The tips of her breasts seared his chest, the sweetest pain he'd ever experienced.

They kissed deeply, and Paul settled over her, shifting his weight to one side so she wouldn't be burdened. His legs straddled hers, placing the most intimate parts of their bodies in heated contact.

"Leah," he breathed into her ear, "I want to make love."

"Paul..."

"I'm not going to hurt you, I swear it."

"I know, but..."

"I'll go nice and slow. I swear by everything I hold dear, I'll stop if you want me to."

Leah smiled sweetly. Dear heaven, everything about her was sweet and delicate. Her gentleness was swallowing him whole. He hadn't intended when he first kissed her to go this far, but she'd been so receptive.

He eased his hand past the band at her waist and downward toward the juncture between her legs. He stroked her thighs until she relaxed and unwittingly opened to him. He claimed her mouth in a heated kiss and at the same moment delved his fingers into the folds of her womanhood. He found her moist and hot . . . and ready.

Leah gasped and nearly came off the bed. "Paul, no."

"Isn't it good?"

"Yes . . . oh yes, only . . ."

"Only what?"

"Don't stop."

Paul laughed softly before kissing her, their mouths dissolving together.

"Leah, I'm going to die if we don't hurry and make love."

She stiffened. Paul silently cursed himself for not being more subtle.

"We can't." She started to squirm under him.

"Why not?" he demanded.

"Because . . . there's someone . . . here."

Only then did Paul hear the persistent peal of the doorbell. "What the hell," he said, bolting off the bed. He didn't bother to reach for his shirt as he marched out of the bedroom and to the front door.

He jerked it open with enough force to pull it off its hinges. Jason stood on the other side—his cap on his head and his bat in his hand.

"What the hell do you want?" Paul snarled.

"Paul," Leah said from somewhere behind him, her voice the cool mist of reason.

"It's Jason," he said, jerking around to face her.

"Don't you think you should invite him in?"

"Frankly, no."

Jason, however, didn't wait for an invitation and boldly strolled into the house. He paused in the middle of the living room and seemed to notice Paul's disheveled state for the first time. Leah was holding together the front of her blouse with both hands, gazing up at his brother with reddened cheeks, wondering too late why she'd ever left the bedroom.

"I don't suppose I've dropped in at an inconvenient time, have I?" Jason asked, grinning ear to ear.

Leah had never been more embarrassed in her entire life. She was sure her cheeks were tomato red.

Jason didn't look the least bit disturbed. Paul looked just plain angry.

Both men, however, were staring at her as if she should be the one to give an explanation. "We're married," she said after an awkward moment.

"Married." Jason's already broad smile widened. "When did this happen?"

Paul looked at his wristwatch. "Three and a half hours ago. You just interrupted my wedding night, little brother. This better be good."

"Anyone else know?" Jason leaned indolently against his baseball bat, crossing his ankles.

"Mom and Dad."

"They've got the children," Leah explained as she turned away. She hurried to the master bedroom and searched for her bra. Her entire face burned with embarrassment. By the time she returned, she had managed to compose herself somewhat.

Jason had plopped himself down on the sectional, resting his ankle on his knee. He looked completely at ease, his arms stretched out beside him.

"So you're married."

"You want to see the proof?" Paul asked.

Jason's gaze meandered over to Leah. "I already have."

Paul's arms circled her waist, bringing her close to his side. "I take it this unexpected visit has a purpose."

"Yeah. But I'm having so much fun watching the color leak in and out of Leah's cheeks that I thought I'd delay getting around to it a bit longer."

"If you value your neck, little brother, you'll get to the point damn soon."

Jason rubbed the side of his jaw. "As I recall, Rich interrupted Christy and Cody's wedding night, too. Must be a family habit."

"Jason."

Paul's brother chuckled and uncrossed his legs. "Actually it's a bit of a bad-news/good-news story."

"Give me the bad news first."

"Harry Duncan, the shortstop you replaced, was hurt this afternoon."

"Playing ball?" Leah hadn't realized softball was so dangerous.

"No," Jason assured her. "He tripped over something in the parking lot and sprained his ankle. It looks like he'll be out for the rest of the season."

"What's the good news?" Paul wanted to know.

"The team has elected you as a permanent replacement."

Leah's heart swelled with pleasure. Paul loved softball. The two weeks he'd played on his brother's team had done him a world of good. He'd come home enthusiastic and happy. She couldn't understand his hesitation now.

"What's the matter?" Jason wanted to know. "I thought you'd be pleased."

"I'm a family man."

"So?" Jason argued. "Rich has got a family, too, and he plays."

Slowly, his face devoid of expression, Paul turned to Leah. "What do you think?"

She nodded eagerly. "I think it'd be wonderful."

"You won't mind?"

"Of course not."

"Then it's settled," Jason said, effortlessly springing to his feet. "I'll go now and let the two of you return to the business of honeymooning." He paused when he reached the front door. "This marriage isn't supposed to be a secret, is it?"

"No." It was Paul who answered.

"Good. Then you won't mind if I tell a few choice folks—like your brother, for instance, Rich, remember? And his wife, Jamie?"

A smile cracked Paul's lips. "I don't mind at all."

"Great. See you two lovebirds later."

Lovebirds. The word leapt out at Leah and slapped her across the face. If Jason hadn't arrived when he did, she and Paul would have made love. Despite all the very good reasons she'd built up in her mind not to. Despite the fact that they weren't in love with one another. Despite the fact that she wasn't emotionally ready to deal with the ramifications of their sleeping together. They would have made love.

Leah walked into the kitchen and stood at the sink, her hands braced against the edge.

Paul followed her.

"I know what you're thinking," he said, standing behind her.

Leah doubted it. "What?"

"You'd prefer it if we waited before making love."

"Yes!" She whirled around to face him. "How'd you know that?"

His smile drooped, lopsided with regret. "Because I think I'd prefer to wait, too."

Paul changed his mind fifteen times in the next fifteen minutes, and a hundred more times as the evening progressed. Jason calling them lovebirds was what convinced him Leah had been right about holding off on the lovemaking.

The word had the same effect as a punch to the stomach. Did he love Leah? Paul didn't know. He was physically hungry for her. Painfully hungry for her. He admired and trusted her. He was grateful to her. He appreciated her. He found her generous, gentle and sweet.

But did he love her?

That was the one question Paul found he couldn't answer. He loved Diane. He could never stop loving her. But if he loved Diane, was it possible to love Leah at the same time?

This was another question for which Paul didn't have the answer.

Although he'd rationalized marriage and a physical relationship between the two of them—Diane wouldn't have wanted him to be alone—he discovered the justification no longer eased his mind. He had no way of really knowing what Diane would have wanted.

Diane had been his wife. But now he was married to Leah. Where the hell did that leave him?

Married to one.

Devoted to the other.

That's where it left him. Exactly where he'd been weeks earlier. One foot in the present, the other in the past. Torn between two sisters.

One alive.

One dead.

Married to both.

Paul took Leah out to dinner that night. A fancy restaurant. Expensive and elegant. He'd already robbed her of so many of the things a wife was entitled to. A courtship, for one.

Leah was a beautiful, generous woman, but she'd been the only one giving in their relationship. It angered Paul that he'd been so oblivious to her needs.

Not only had Leah been deprived of courtship, but she hadn't even had a decent wedding—a ceremony with flowers and music, family and friends. Instead he'd rushed her to a preacher friend, not even the minister from the church they attended. He'd married her before a stranger, as though he were ashamed.

As the evening progressed, Paul felt even more of a louse. He'd cheated this warm, gracious woman out of so much. He wondered how long it would take him to make it up to her. He knew one thing. He would do it long before he'd make any physical demands on her.

Leah deserved that much.

Leah wasn't sure what she should expect out of marriage to Paul. After the first week of married life, she was more confused than ever. Other than that first afternoon, Paul had barely touched her. He kissed her cheek before he left for the office and again when he arrived home. But that was the extent of their physical contact.

Yet he'd never been more generous to her. He was constantly bringing her small gifts. A red rose on Monday. Bubble bath on Wednesday. A huge chocolate chip cookie on Friday.

Leah didn't know what to make of the changes in him. He was patient and gentle. Tender in ways she hadn't expected. He took time to praise her efforts, compliment her on the way she looked and on how clean the house was or how happy the children seemed.

This was all well and good. But Leah longed to be a wife. A real wife. Not just a stand-in wife and mother, a replacement for her sister.

She wanted to be loved for herself. Appreciated for being the woman she was, not because Paul felt she'd made some noble sacrifice for him and the children.

Nights were the worst time for Leah. After dinner Paul generally worked on his novel. He waited until the children were in bed—he'd always been wonderful in that respect, helping her with the twins and Kelsey. But as soon as they were down for the evening, he retreated to his den.

Although he'd never said as much, not that he ever would, Leah was convinced his sudden interest in the novel was a convenient way to escape being alone with her.

It might not have hurt so much if he hadn't kissed her and loved her so sweetly the first afternoon they were married. If he hadn't kissed her and told her how beautiful she was to him, she might never have known what she was missing.

But she did know.

Perhaps she'd done something wrong. Perhaps a woman wasn't supposed to have made the sounds she made or have liked the things he'd done as much as she had. Perhaps Paul had been put off by her reactions. If she wasn't such a coward, she'd ask him. Instead she was tormented night after night by his presence. They slept in the same bed, but they might as well be in different countries for all the space Paul maintained between them.

All three of the children could have slept comfortably between them. And sometimes they had.

Ryan and Ronnie were pleased that their aunt Leah was now their daddy's wife. Leah wasn't completely sure they understood the implication, except that she'd moved into the bedroom with their dad and they could have their playroom back.

Nearly two weeks after their wedding, Leah was convinced Paul never intended to make love to her. She was busy arranging a vase of cut flowers after dinner one evening when Paul came into the kitchen. The kids were sleeping, and the night was gentle and warm.

Paul poured himself a cup of coffee.

"How's the writing going?" she asked, keeping up the facade.

"Slow."

"Do you want to talk over the scene?" They did that sometimes.

"No."

His refusal hurt a little. If he hadn't been so good to her in so many other ways lately, Leah would have felt even worse. She gave him a smile for encouragement and returned to her task.

A half hour later she was coming out of the bathroom and into the hallway—her hair damp, wearing a cool cotton gown—just as Paul came in from the kitchen. He stopped when he saw her. His blue eyes widened and went a bit wild.

Neither moved.

Leah could see every breath he drew. She watched the pulse hammer in his neck and felt the tension that seemed to pulse through his body.

In that minute Leah knew he wanted her. It wasn't tension that pulsed through him but desire.

"Paul," she whispered, holding her hand out to him, "I . . . I want you."

She might have hit him for the reaction he gave. He closed his eyes as though struggling within himself. "You're sure?"

She nodded. "I'm ready to be your wife."

"There'll be no turning back."

"I know."

He took one step toward her and she met him halfway. He wrapped his arms around her waist and lifted her from the floor until her mouth was level with his own. Then he kissed her, with an urgency that knocked the breath from her lungs.

Chapter Nine

Leah's mouth was warm, moist and gentle. Paul's arms, gripping her about the waist, lifted her, leaving her feet dangling just above the floor. He continued kissing her and at the same time carried her into their bedroom, closing the door with his foot.

He was trembling he was so eager. His hands and his heart both. Taking in deep breaths, Paul tried to make himself go slow and easy. For days he'd been waiting for her to make some small sign. A look would have satisfied him. A word. A sigh.

Anything.

But until now he'd found no encouragement from Leah.

In the past two weeks Paul had tried to court her, show her how much he appreciated her. How grateful he was to have her in his life. He'd made an effort to bring her small gifts. But the tokens seemed insignificant to everything that was in his heart. If anything, the gifts he brought her embarrassed her more than they pleased her.

He wanted to talk openly with her, explain all that was on his mind, but found it impossible. To his credit, the first week of courting her the way she deserved, his motives had been pure and good. It was torture sleeping with her at his side and not touching her. No small feat, he realized, particularly now that he held her in his arms.

The second week his vision of what he had hoped to accomplish had blurred; his objective had obscured behind a growing physical need. Soon he'd lost track of just about everything, except what he was so foolishly denying himself. At night he closed himself off in his den, because being alone with her and not touching her was next to impossible then.

Now that she was voluntarily in his arms, Paul wanted no room for misunderstanding. This time what they started, they would finish. There was no turning back once she gave herself to him. He wanted there to be no room for doubt, no room for regret.

His hands were eager as he stripped off her cotton nightgown. He discarded his own clothes while Leah turned back the sheets. Her back was to him, and he marveled once more at the perfection he saw in her. The simple, elegant beauty that was hers. She was exquisite, beautiful enough to steal his breath away. Beautiful enough to heal his heart and give him a reason to live again.

She must have sensed his warm perusal because she paused in her task and turned back to him. Her gaze shyly skirted past him as she smiled weakly. Paul reached out and pressed his hand against her face, and she cocked her head slightly to one side and pressed her own hand over his.

"Second thoughts?"

Her gaze dropped as she shook her head. "None."

"Good." Which had to be the understatement of the century. He reached for her, gathering her in his arms, loving the feel of her hands flattened against his back. The feel of her breasts caressing his bare chest. The fuzzy warmth of her womanhood cradling the solid length of his sex.

Her touch was electric, warming him, reminding him he was alive. More alive than he could ever remember being. He wanted to take this slowly for fear of frightening her with the strength of his desire, but he didn't know if it was possible.

He laid her on the bed and knelt above her, kissing her, hoping to disguise the urgency of his need. The atmosphere was alive with wonder, vivid with sensation. Her mouth felt like velvet, her kiss rich and delicious.

The harsh realities of life that had been haunting him for months seemed to disappear. The emotions and doubts that had plagued him since their marriage melted into the night.

All that was left between them was the warm richness of their desire for one another. All that was left was a beauty that transcended everything about him, an inner light that guided him.

When he positioned himself above her, Leah opened to him and gently raised her hips, putting her moist softness in contact with the thick, hard length of his erection.

"You're so hot," she whispered.

Paul felt himself tremble. Every instinct within him demanded that he sink into her, yet he restrained himself, wanting to pleasure her in a hundred different ways before he sought completion.

Her hands were braced against his shoulders as she arched upward a second time, and Paul found it impossible to wait a moment longer. With one swift stroke he buried himself into the satin heat of her.

The pleasure was so keen Paul thought he would die with it. He paused when he saw her biting into her lower lip, and cursed his impatience, fearing he might have been too rough for her.

"I hurt you?"

Her beautiful eyes drifted open, hazy with passion. Gradually a smile came to her lips, a radiant, happy smile. "No... this isn't anything even close to pain."

"I'm not going to last long," he warned her, gritting his teeth.

In response she smiled anew, closed her eyes and gently buckled beneath him.

"Leah... don't." He called out her name at the intense pleasure she gave him, fearing he wouldn't endure another second of such keen pleasure with her moving beneath him.

He began to move slowly of his own accord, gliding out, pausing just a moment, then fully sheathing himself into her warmth once more. He marveled at the display of expressions that flickered across her face. He viewed her wonder, her joy and perhaps most keenly, her pleasure. It was the sight of her completion that produced his own.

Rarely had Paul experienced anything more beautiful than he did with those few minutes with Leah. His heart burned with love, but he dared not voice his feelings. Not now, not after they'd made love for the first time; she might confuse his confession with gratitude for the pleasures they'd found together. She didn't know the gratitude that saturated his heart.

He leaned forward and pressed his cheek to hers, his breath coming in labored gasps. Her own breath was as halting as his, her arms wrapped around his neck.

Thinking he was too heavy for her, he went to move, but Leah stopped him.

"Stay inside me a little longer."

He hesitated. "You're sure?"

"Very."

He kissed her, thoroughly, sweeping in the inside of her mouth with his tongue, loving her for surrounding him with her gentleness and her warmth.

"Oh, Paul," she whispered, her eyes bright with tears. "I never realized it could be so beautiful." She combed her fingers through his hair and brought his head down to her breast. "I didn't think you were ever going to want to make love to me."

"Me not make...not want...never going to..." The words twisted themselves around the end of his tongue, confusing him. "I've been doing everything but cartwheels in an effort to get you to notice me. What do you need, woman, smoke signals?"

Leah chuckled softly. "I doubt if it would have done any good."

"Why not?"

"Because I've discovered, for all your brilliance, you can be pretty dense."

"Who? Me?"

"If anyone needed to send up smoke signals, it was me."

Paul was floored. "Are you trying to tell me you've... you wanted me?"

She nodded. "I tried to say something... but, you kept avoiding me."

"Avoiding you?" He couldn't believe his ears. "I had to escape because I didn't trust myself alone with you. Leah, dear God, I've been crazy for you for weeks."

"You have?"

It amazed him how genuinely surprised she was to hear it. "You've kept me waiting nearly two weeks." His gaze wandered to her plump breast and, although he had been thoroughly satisfied only moments before, he experienced a fierce need to taste her.

"I'm... not very good at letting you know my feelings, am I?"

"Don't worry about it," he said, sliding his hand down to her breast.

"Paul?"

"Hmm?" he answered absently. He was intrigued by her breasts, their roundness, their rose-colored crests. He examined them, weighing one in his palm, fondling it, loving the feel of it in his hand. He ran his thumb over the peak until it pouted, firm and flushed.

Leah's hips made a small, almost involuntary movement, drawing him deeper inside her.

"You wanted something?" he asked, smiling down on her. "Remember I'm not a mind reader. You're

going to have to tell me what it is you want." He was
hard again, harder than he had been originally, though
he'd thought it impossible. His tongue flickered over
her nipple, then took her full into his mouth and
sucked softly, then, not so softly.

"Yes." She was biting into her lower lip, her eyes
closed. Her hips came off the bed, rising to meet him,
to silently implore him for more.

Paul paused and raised his head. "You wanted
something?"

"Yes ... oh, yes."

"Good. Just tell me what it is you want."

"Paul ... I want you."

The walls of her femininity closed around him like a
tight fist. She sighed when he began to move, height-
ening his arousal until he filled her completely. With
her eyes closed, she moaned at his first powerful thrust,
rising up to meet him. Opening herself to him, loving
him until he felt humbled in the wake of her generosity and her love.

At work Paul's mind wandered. There was probably a word for what was happening between him and
Leah; he just didn't know what it was. Paul had never
wanted to make love to a woman as frequently as he
did Leah. They'd finish, and not a minute would pass
before he'd think about making love to her again. It
worried him, it troubled him, but try as he might, Paul
could come up with no explanation for the deep physical hunger she aroused in him.

Simply put, he needed Leah. He experienced free-
dom in making love to her and joy. A joy so deep it all
but sang from his heart. He expected to be left to deal

with remorse and guilt, and had been almost giddy with relief when he felt neither. The first night he'd made love to her he had lain awake and waited for the guilt to come crashing in on him. It hadn't.

Frankly he wasn't certain what he should be feeling. Naturally there was a tremendous physical relief. It had been nearly a year since he'd made love. When they finally did crash through the barriers, Paul had half expected the guilt to swallow him in giant waves. He had expected to feel something.

If not guilt, then what?

He had loved Diane. He loved her still. That confused him even more. If he cared so deeply for Diane, then how was it possible for him to love Leah as much as he did? One more question for which Paul had no answer.

He didn't want to think too intensely, or pry too deeply into his psyche. Heaven only knew what he might manage to dig up. He didn't want to flirt with guilt, didn't want to give it a toehold in his marriage to Leah.

Questioning the happiness he'd found might destroy what they had, and Paul didn't want to risk that. For the first time in months he was feeling something other than emotional pain, and it felt good. It felt damn good. He didn't want to do anything that might take away the happiness Leah had brought into his soul.

Just thinking about his wife, at home waiting for him, made Paul rush out of the office. He found he did that most evenings now, eager to get home to his family. He'd hug his children, and then bide his time until he could make love to his wife, to Leah.

Tonight he could barely wait for the kids to go to sleep after dinner. When they protested saying it was still light outside, Paul appeased the twins by reading them a story. He tucked them in bed and waited a few minutes to be sure they were sleeping.

Then he walked into the kitchen. Leah glanced over to him and smiled shyly. Paul gave her his special look, and she knew what he had in mind. The same thing he'd had in mind every night for the past week.

There was a sweet innocence about her that got to him. Really got to him. He'd look at her in a certain way, and she'd blush. Heavens, how Paul loved to make her blush. Watching the color flood her face entranced him. This evening was no exception.

"Leah." He moved up behind her and slipped his arms around her waist. He nuzzled her neck, marveling at how powerfully he could desire her. "Let's go to bed."

"Paul, I think we should talk."

"Later," he promised, kissing the side of her neck. "We'll do all the talking you want later. I promise." His hands found her breasts, and he smiled triumphantly at the way they peaked against his palms in ready response.

"The boys... they just went down."

"They're asleep. I made sure of that."

"But..."

He was vaguely surprised by her slight resistance. Not once since that first night had she offered even a token protest. He slipped his hand under her blouse and fondled her breast.

"We shouldn't... it's barely eight."

"Yes, I know," he said, finding her ear and sucking gently at the lobe. "Am I embarrassing you?"

"No... It's just, I'd...I'd feel better if we had a talk...first."

"Do you mind if we chat just a tad later? I fear my mind is on more pressing details."

"I...don't know." She sounded hesitant, unsure.

Paul told himself he should have stopped then, but his arousal fit so snugly against her.... With such important matters demanding his attention, he was hard-pressed to...

He turned her around, and their mouths dissolved in a warm, wet kiss.

"I'm not even done with the dinner dishes," she complained.

"I'll help you...later." He kissed her again, slowly, leisurely, her kiss reeling his senses. "Leah..." he pleaded, "for the love of heaven, let's go to bed."

"What do you want?"

Her question took him by storm. What did he want? He couldn't have made it more obvious. "I want you."

"Are you sure?" She refused to look at him.

"Yes. I want to make love to you. This shouldn't come as a surprise to you, Leah. We've been making love regularly for a week now."

"Eight days straight."

"Good, you're keeping track." He urged her toward the bedroom, but she resisted. "All right," he said, dragging in a deep breath. "What's wrong?"

"I...don't know."

Paul nearly ground his teeth in frustration, trying his best not to behave like a beast, trying to give her all the time she needed. "Obviously something's troubling you."

"Yes..." She turned around, apparently unwilling to face him. "What about Diane?"

His shoulders sagged. "What about her?"

When she spoke, her voice was low and hoarse with pain. "Do you... do you pretend..."

"No." He didn't allow her to finish because he knew what she was going to ask. "Not once have I made love to you and thought of her. Not once." He said it emphatically, so there would be no doubt in her mind.

"Then... then what *do* you think about?"

He said the first thing that came to him. The truth. "How much I want you, how much you satisfy me. How grateful I am you're in my life and in my bed."

She opened her eyes and slowly raised her gaze to his, reading his expression, seeking some outward sign that he was telling her the truth.

His hand reached for hers, and he raised her knuckles to his lips. "It's true, Leah. It's you I want."

He kissed her then, amazed, not for the first time, at how sweet her kiss was. How potent. He silently cheered at the ready response he felt in her. She melted in his arms and moaned softly.

"You're sure the boys are asleep?" she asked in a whisper-thin voice.

"I made sure of it," Paul said, urging her toward the bedroom. His heart beat with renewed excitement when she didn't hesitate. "Is there anything else you want to know?"

"No." She was eager now, too. Paul could feel it and it fueled his own excitement.

Within seconds they were in the bedroom with the door firmly closed. Paul hurriedly undressed, and when he'd finished he helped Leah out of her things. When their clothing was little more than two piles on the floor, Paul reached for her, kissing her hungrily, starving for her.

She was so beautiful. Her breasts were perfect, her legs long and shapely. His thoughts wandered to the shadowed delta between her legs, and he knew in that moment he had to have her soon. He reached for the lamp, intending to turn it off.

"Leave it on," she whispered, stopping him.

His eyes mated with hers, and he read her fears. He smiled and nodded, gently placing her on the bed. Leah's arms reached out to him, and with a sigh he claimed his wife. Claimed her love. Claimed her heart.

Replete, his wife in his arms, Paul soaked in the warm magic that was his after making love to Leah. He held her hand in his own, fingers entwined, needing to maintain the connection between them. He longed to hold on to the pleasure she gave him for as long as he could. The physical pleasure, yes, but also the mental, the spiritual high he experienced, along with the carnal.

"I embarrass you, don't I?" he asked her candidly.

"Embarrass me?"

"Wanting to make love to you as often as I do."

Her smile widened, and the fingers of her free hand inched across his chest. "I don't understand it...I guess I'm afraid of it."

"Afraid?"

"That it's only a temporary thing...that you'll wake up some morning and realize it's me you're married to and not my sister. And then everything will come to an end..."

"Leah." Her words shattered his peace. He sat up, supporting himself on his elbow. "You didn't need to leave the light on for me to know it was you I was making love to. You don't need to be afraid that I don't know who you are." He paused and captured her mouth, kissing her, but stopping himself before the kiss became sensual or demanding. "I know you're my wife. I thank God for you each and every day."

Leah hesitated. "I shouldn't have said any-thing...shouldn't have mentioned it."

"No, I'm glad you did," he countered, drawing her even closer to his side, marveling at the way her body molded itself to his own. "I don't want you to doubt. If I wasn't so dense, I would have said something my-self a whole lot sooner. I didn't realize...didn't think."

"My mind plays crazy tricks on me sometimes," she confessed softly.

"On me, too, but not once have I ever confused you with Diane. I need you, Leah. Not because we make beautiful love together, and not because of all the help you've given me with the children, either. I don't know when it happened or even why, but I need you in my life. To laugh with me. To share the joy of raising my children, to share the grief of having lost someone we both deeply loved."

Paul's hands abandoned hers and gently moved to brush away the hair from her face. "I call myself a writer, work with words every day, yet I find myself at a loss for them now. I wish I could say everything I feel for you. I wish I could explain what's in my heart in a sweet, romantic way... the way you deserve.''

"It isn't romance I need.''

"I want you, Leah. I need you. I thank God for you every day.''

His mouth took hers, and sighing, she raised her arms and looped them around his neck.

The phone on the bedside table rang just then, and Paul groaned and broke away. He let it ring a second time in an effort to compose himself before answering.

"Hello.'' Despite his best efforts he sounded gruff and impatient.

"Paul, it's Rich. Have you got a minute?''

Paul's gaze linked with Leah's and he grinned. That was about as long as he could spare. "Yeah, a minute.''

"Jamie and I were just talking. Actually Jason was in on the discussion, too.''

"What discussion?''

"I'm getting around to that, so quit being so impatient. We all want to take you and Leah out to dinner Saturday night. Sort of a welcome-to-the-family thing for Leah. We should have done it sooner, but with Mom and Dad out of town, it slipped our minds.''

It took an instant for his brother's words to sink in. He turned his face away from his wife because looking at Leah—her lips swollen and moist, her breasts pouting up at him—was too distracting.

"What did you say?''

"Dinner. Saturday night for you and Leah. Are you sure you don't want me to phone back later?''

"I'm sure...we'll need to find a sitter, but that shouldn't be much of a problem."

"I know Mom and Dad will want to hold a reception for the two of you once they're back from Montana, but that's likely to be a month or more."

"Or longer."

"Exactly," Rich concurred. "It's too long to wait. We all like Leah and want to be sure she feels welcome."

"That's very nice."

A short silence stretched between them while Paul tried to think of an excuse to get off the phone.

"You might want to check with Leah," Rich suggested. "She may have made some other plans."

"Oh...right." Paul realized he probably sounded like a major dunce. "Hold on a minute." He cupped his hand over the receiver. "It's Rich. He's inviting us out to dinner Saturday evening. Is that a problem?"

"Ah...not that I can think of."

"It's fine," he said. "I'll see you Saturday, then." He was prepared to hang up the receiver when Rich stopped him.

"You might be interested in knowing what time."

"Oh, right." He opened his bed-stand drawer and reached for a pen, then wrote down the necessary information.

There was a slight hesitation from Rich once he'd finished. "Are you all right, Paul? You don't sound like yourself."

"I'm fine," he answered as evenly as possible. He hung up the phone a minute later, and without pausing reached for Leah. "Now, where were we?"

* * *

Leah had always enjoyed Jamie, Rich's wife. But until Paul had joined the softball team, she'd only talked to her sister-in-law briefly. Whenever she did, Leah had been impressed by how charming and gracious Jamie was. She didn't know her well enough to confide in her, but she hoped that some day in the future she would.

Leah needed a friend. Now more than ever. Diane was gone, and she'd drifted away from Linda, whose life had become so much different than her own now.

It wouldn't surprise Leah to learn that the Saturday dinner had been Jamie's idea. The two women had met briefly earlier in the week. Jamie had a doctor's appointment and her usual baby-sitter hadn't been able to watch Bethany, so she'd contacted Leah. Naturally Leah had been happy to do it.

She should have mentioned it to Jamie then, but she hadn't. It hadn't seemed right at the time to be talking to her sister-in-law about matters that were between a husband and a wife. Matters a husband knew nothing about.

It hadn't been the least bit of trouble taking Bethany for those few hours, and Jamie had seemed so grateful. She'd returned from the doctor's appointment beaming with the news of a second pregnancy. Leah hadn't told Paul, not wanting to ruin Rich's good news.

Perhaps it was Jamie's happy news that brought Diane to mind. Leah missed her sister, but not nearly as often now as she had in the beginning. Nevertheless Diane still stood, bold as ever, between her and Paul. Between her and the children.

Although Paul had been quick to offer her reassurances that Diane's presence hadn't followed them into the bedroom, Leah's fears weren't completely laid to rest. Maybe Paul was telling her the truth. Leah longed to believe that Diane wasn't a part of their lovemaking, but if that was the case then why did Leah wrestle with so much guilt afterward?

No matter how often they made love, she struggled with that one emotion—guilt. Without ever really meaning for it to happen, she truly had taken her sister's place.

Although the children called her Leah, they thought of her as their mother. As Paul's mother had pointed out to her in a recent conversation, Leah was the only mother Kelsey had ever known.

She was a wife to Paul, too. A wife in every way. But Leah wasn't fooling herself. She knew her sister was really the children's mother. Although he had married her, Paul didn't love her. Maybe he wanted her, something he confessed to often. Maybe he needed her, something he demonstrated frequently. But he didn't love her. Not the way he had Diane.

Leah had thought she'd be content marrying Paul to raise the twins and Kelsey as her own children. A husband and a family were more than she'd ever dreamed of having. But, to her dismay, she found herself becoming greedy.

The realization came heavy to her heart. She would always be a substitute. A poor second. A stand-in wife and mother.

Perhaps she was feeling sorry for herself. It wasn't like her to feel so melancholy, or so morose, but she was carrying an additional burden of late.

It didn't make sense that taking her sister's place should so suddenly be bothering Leah so much. Not when she'd been living with Paul nearly three months, married to him a month of that time.

Admit it, her heart cried. You're in love with him.

So what if I am.

He loves Diane.

That's all right, you loved Diane, too. She asked you to take her place, remember?

Leah did remember, but she hadn't expected to fall in love with Paul. Hadn't expected her heart to become involved. Hadn't expected so many things.

She dressed carefully for the Saturday dinner, wanting Paul to be proud of her, but knowing no matter what she wore or how she did her hair, she would never be as beautiful as Diane.

Paul was in and out of the bedroom while she dressed. She'd been looking forward to this evening all week. Now she wasn't so sure.

She'd been feeling listless all day, yet pleased, also tired and a bit despondent. At noon she'd lain down with the kids and napped. Leah couldn't remember the last time she'd taken a nap. Not since she'd first moved in with Paul, at any rate.

"You ready?" he asked, walking into their bedroom.

"I will be in a few more minutes."

Paul hesitated. "Are you feeling all right?"

She nodded, holding back her news. All her life she'd been terrible about keeping secrets.

"You're not feeling well, are you?"

She sat at the edge of the mattress and reached for her shoe, slipping on the patent leather pump, biding her time. She hadn't meant to say anything, at least not yet.

"Did I tell you I watched Bethany the other day for Jamie while she went to the doctor?" she asked, her voice low and uneven.

"I seem to remember you saying something about it. Why?"

"No reason." She chickened out, not wanting to ruin the evening for them both.

"Leah, what's wrong?"

"Nothing." She wiped her hand under her eye for fear she might soon start weeping. "I've been feeling...different all day."

"Any special reason?" He sat on the bed beside her and reached for her hand.

Leah shrugged.

"Rich tells me Jamie's expecting again."

Leah nodded. "I'm real pleased for them."

"Better them than us," Paul said with a small laugh.

Leah froze and withdrew her hand from his. "What makes you say that?" she asked defensively.

"For obvious reasons."

"I see," she said stiffly.

"What do you see?" How puzzled he sounded, how perplexed.

There was no holding back the truth now. "Did it ever occur to you that...that I might be pregnant, too?"

Chapter Ten

"Are you pregnant?" Paul demanded. He couldn't seem to stand still. His heart was in his throat, and the *fear* ... the all-consuming fear branded his soul. He stuffed his hands in his pants pockets and formed tight fists.

"Are you?" he demanded a second time when Leah didn't immediately respond.

"I don't know."

He jerked one hand free and raked it through his hair with enough force to jerk back his head. "How could something like this have happened?"

Leah looked so small, sitting there on the edge of the mattress, her head lowered. His question appeared to revive her. Slowly, her hazel eyes burning with indignation, she raised her gaze to his. "What do you mean, how could something like this have happened? Think about it, Paul. Just think about it."

"We've been careful."

"What . . . what about the first time?"

He uttered an oath, short and to the point. Then, seeing Leah flinch, his regret was instantaneous. He would have given his right arm to have yanked back the ugly word. That first night they'd made love had been incredibly beautiful, one of the most beautiful experiences of his life. But the thought that their first time together might have borne fruit terrified him to the marrow of his bones.

"There was one other time, too . . . remember?" she informed him quietly, having composed herself.

Paul did remember. He'd been so damn eager for her they hadn't taken the necessary precautions. "How late are you?" he asked after a moment.

"Six days."

"Oh God." Diane had never been late, except when she had been carrying the twins and Kelsey. She had always known by the end of first week of her missed period whether or not she was pregnant.

"I . . . I'm not generally late, but . . . I could be for one reason or another."

Paul nodded, but he wasn't listening. His mind was whirling like a helicopter blade as he thought back over the past couple of days. Leah had seemed overly tired and listless. Diane had been the same way the first trimester of her pregnancies.

His heart froze in his chest, the dread nearly devouring him. Dear God, he couldn't lose Leah. Not his wife. Not again. He couldn't bear it; he couldn't sur-

vive without Leah. Not now, when he was just beginning to live again.

"I...I made an appointment with the doctor for first
thing Monday morning," she said haltingly. "I wasn't
going to say anything until I'd been in to see him...but
it's been on my mind and..."

"You should have said something long before this."

"Why?" she flared. "So you could be angry with me
sooner?"

"I'm not angry."

"You're not exactly overjoyed, either."

"You're right," he answered crossly, "I'm not. Can
you blame me?"

"No." The lone word was a strangled whisper. Her
chin came up and tears brimmed her eyes, ready to spill
down her ashen cheeks. Her lower lip started to tremble, and Paul felt a knife twist in his heart.

She was vulnerable, sitting there, pale and beautiful, bleeding from the wounds his fear had inflicted.
He knelt down in front of her and took her hands in his
own. Drawing in a deep breath, he closed his eyes and
took a moment to collect himself. "I'm sorry, Leah. I
didn't mean to raise my voice. Whatever happens, we'll
deal with it together. All right?"

She nodded.

The doorbell chimed in the distance, and Paul knew
it was the baby-sitter. "Are you ready?"

Once more Leah nodded. "I think so...I'm
sorry...my timing is incredibly bad...I shouldn't have
mentioned it tonight...it just sort of slipped out."

Paul kissed her temple and placed his hand upon her
shoulder. "We'll talk about it later. For now let's put
it behind us and enjoy our dinner. Agreed?"

She gave him a watery smile and nodded.

* * *

Leah didn't know how she was going to survive the dinner with Paul's family. With everything in her, she wished she hadn't mentioned the possibility of her being pregnant to Paul. The thought had been growing within her for the past couple of days, so she'd already walked through a full spectrum of emotions. It hadn't been fair to hit Paul with the news so unexpectedly, right before a dinner party.

When she'd first realized the possibility, Leah's immediate reaction had been sheer joy. She'd been standing in front of the calendar in the kitchen and checking the dates when the realization struck her. It didn't seem possible. So soon. They'd only made love a few times and yet... and yet it seemed the most logical explanation for why she was late.

Her heart had nearly burst, she was so excited. Her timing wasn't exactly spectacular—they'd only been married a few weeks—but that shouldn't matter. She loved Paul and the thought of nurturing his child, their child, had filled her with an incredible joy.

She'd been a bit fearful, too. Not because of what had happened to her sister. Diane's death had come about through a rare series of events. The likelihood of its repeating itself was so slim it didn't warrant consideration. What did concern her were the demands of another child. She loved Kelsey and the twins dearly, but by the end of the day she was exhausted.

But her biggest fear had been Paul's reaction to her news. For that reason alone she hadn't intended to mention a baby to him until she was certain. She hadn't meant to say anything. She certainly hadn't intended to blurt it out the way she had. Perhaps she was hoping, praying, he'd share some of her happiness.

Only Paul hadn't been happy. He'd been furious. Then regretful. In many ways she could understand and forgive his reaction; nevertheless it hurt. The pain went so deep, Leah didn't know how she was going to sit through dinner and smile when her heart was breaking.

"How often have you been late before?" Paul asked once they were in the car.

"Not often, and never more than a few days... that I can remember."

His hands tightened on the steering wheel until his knuckles went white. "I was afraid of that."

"I... thought you said we shouldn't worry about it now."

He sighed, a sound filled with self-derision. "You're right, but damn it all, I don't know if I can stop thinking about it."

Leah waited a moment, her heart aching. "Would it be so terrible?"

"Yes." His response was immediate and harsh.

Leah's throat constricted. She turned her head and looked out the side window, wondering how she was going to keep from weeping. It wouldn't hurt nearly as badly if she didn't know how Paul had reacted when Diane had told him she was pregnant with the twins, or when they'd learned she was going to have Kelsey. Paul had been thrilled. Exuberant. He'd been so excited the two had celebrated for weeks. Diane had claimed Paul loved her the most when she was pregnant. He was gentle and romantic.

With Diane.

With Leah he was angry and disappointed.

Unexpectedly Paul reached for her hand, gripping it. "Don't worry, we'll get through this."

"I'm not the one who's worried."

From the corner of her eye, Leah watched as Paul's features tightened. "Maybe you should be."

"Why?"

"Why?" he exploded. "You just don't get it, do you? Look what happened to Diane when she had Kelsey. Do you honestly think I want to lose you?"

"A pregnancy isn't going to kill me."

"I don't want to chance it," he said firmly, leaving no room for discussion.

"Unfortunately we may not have the option."

His lips tightened. "Do you mind if we deal with this some other time? We're nearly at the restaurant."

"All right," she whispered, by some miracle managing to hold the tears at bay.

When they arrived Jason was sitting in the restaurant foyer waiting for them. Leah could have sworn it was the first time she'd seen Paul's brother without a baseball cap on his head. He was tall and good-looking. His eyes were the same intense shade of blue as Paul's. He stood and smiled when they entered the restaurant.

"I see you two made it," Jason said. "Rich and Jamie will be here any minute."

Paul's smile lacked just about everything. He buried his hands in his pockets and stared across the linen-covered tables to the view of Lake Union.

"So, Leah," Jason said, apparently willing to try again, "how's married life treating you?"

"Fine." There was no need to exaggerate.

Jason hesitated. "I'm pleased to hear it."

Leah, too, focused her gaze in the distance. The ability to make small talk had deserted her completely.

"Jamie made reservations earlier in the week," Jason announced. "Why don't we wait for them at our table? We might as well relax a bit and enjoy the view."

"Sounds like a good idea to me." Paul was the one who spoke. He pressed his hand at the small of Leah's back as they followed the hostess to a table for six at the window.

"Will someone else be joining us?" Leah asked conversationally, hoping to make up for her lack earlier. "A date, Jason?"

"Not for me," he said, reaching toward the middle of the table for a celery stick. "I'm leaving all the marrying in this family to everyone else."

"Don't you want to marry?"

"Yes and no...I'm not opposed to it, but it definitely isn't in my game plan."

"I understand what you mean," Leah said, reaching for an olive, ignoring Paul, who sat silent and morose next to her. She'd felt much the same way until she'd moved in with Paul and the children. "It would be nice if it happened, but if you don't find someone it won't be the end of the world."

"Exactly."

Paul remained ominously silent.

A couple of moments later Rich and Jamie arrived. Jamie's eyes were bright with happiness. Rich scooted out the chair for his wife, his gaze holding hers as the two exchanged a lover's look.

They took a few minutes to greet one another and then they all studied the menu. "Tonight's a dual celebration," Rich announced proudly, smiling toward his wife. "As you probably already know, Jamie and I are going to be parents for the second time."

"All right," Jason said, grinning proudly.

"Congratulations," Leah said, continuing to study her menu.

"Congratulations," Paul echoed with a decided lack of enthusiasm.

If anyone noticed, and Leah prayed they hadn't, they didn't comment. Watching Rich and Jamie and seeing the love they shared so openly, so generously with one another, Leah felt her heart ache anew.

She hadn't thought she could have been any more miserable than she already was, but sitting through dinner with Paul's brother and his wife was pure torture. The love Rich and Jamie shared was like a mirror that reflected all the weaknesses in Leah's relationship with Paul. His reaction to the news that she might be pregnant confirmed everything she'd ever feared about her marriage. Everything she'd feared about his love for her. She was married to him, but she was only a stand-in wife and a stand-in mother.

They ordered their meal and a bottle of wine to honor love; at least that was what Jason suggested. But Leah didn't feel much like celebrating and apparently Paul didn't, either. For the second time that evening, Leah prayed no one noticed. She wasn't worried about Rich and Jamie feeling slighted. Their attention was focused on one another, but Jason was another story. More than once she felt her brother-in-law's gaze probing her. She tried to smile, tried to reassure him, but Leah discovered she had relatively few reassurances to give.

Not once did Paul speak directly to her during their dinner. Leah didn't know if the slight was intentional or not. He hadn't spoken to anyone else, either, she noticed, unless he was directly addressed.

The entire evening was a disaster. Leah fully accepted the blame. She should never have told Paul about the baby when she had...if there even was a baby.

"You barely touched your dinner," her husband commented on the drive home.

"I...wasn't hungry."

Silence filled the car. An uncomfortable silence that was punctuated by the even rhythm of their misery.

"You didn't seem much interested in eating yourself."

Paul forcefully expelled his breath. "I guess I wasn't hungry, either."

For the life of him Paul couldn't sleep. Guilt and fear made for hellish bed companions. He'd never thought of himself as a particularly heroic man, but he wasn't a coward, either. From the minute Leah announced she might be pregnant, that opinion of himself had been revised.

He was the biggest coward who ever lived. He'd trembled with fear from the moment the word *pregnancy* escaped her lips.

Knowing it was useless to toss and turn any longer, Paul climbed out of bed and made his way into the kitchen. He didn't turn on the lights, but pulled out a chair and sat down in the dark. Propping his elbows against the tabletop, he buried his face in his hands and tried to reason with himself.

He should have been more careful, he told himself. He was an adult. He knew how to prevent a pregnancy. In light of what had happened to Diane, his carelessness, his casual neglect of precautions, amazed him.

He loved Leah, honestly loved her. Their love-making was incredible, and always had been. He didn't think a man could be gifted with a more perfect wife. In bed and out. He didn't understand how he could have been so fortunate as to have married two of the most generous, loving women he'd ever known. *Two*. But only one was with him now.

He couldn't lose Leah. He didn't have whatever it took to live through losing her. He couldn't bury another wife.

The memory of the night Diane had died came to him. He recalled Dr. Charman's words, so stark and cold, as he told Paul how sorry he was, how he'd done everything possible to save her. He'd gone on to explain exactly what had happened, but by that point Paul hadn't been listening. All he'd heard was that his wife was gone.

A fresh wave of grief came over him, hitting him with the impact of a tidal wave.

He couldn't lose Leah. Dear God, not again. Not again.

Not for the first time Paul realized how selfish and self-centered he'd been when it came to Leah. Without ever intending to, he'd slighted her in so many ways.

He was just beginning to deal with the news of her pregnancy, accept it, face his fears and prepare to speak openly with her, when he'd heard her talking to Jason about marriage. Leah had never expected to marry, she'd told his brother, and hadn't looked for it to happen. She had sounded so blasé about their marriage, so flippant. Her attitude had stunned him.

Here he was, so crazy in love with her that he wore his heart on his sleeve like a schoolboy. He had assumed he was well past the point of having his feelings hurt. Nevertheless her words had hurt him.

Perhaps he was overreacting; Paul didn't know anymore. He loved her, and she'd made their marriage sound as though he'd just happened to stumble into her life. As if she'd only accepted his proposal because she wasn't likely to get another.

Maybe if he hadn't been so worried about her being pregnant, he might not have taken the comment so personally. Paul wasn't sure about that, either.

His thoughts churned in his mind for endless hours until dawn crept over the horizon. Somewhere near morning he returned to bed and crawled between the covers, gathering Leah close in his arms, needing her warmth to chase away the chill that had gripped his heart.

Monday morning Paul came out of the bedroom dressed for work, while Leah was cooking breakfast for Kelsey and the boys. Ryan and Ronnie were busy setting the table, and Kelsey was in her high chair, batting about her cup and singing cheerfully.

Not once since they'd left the restaurant had Paul mentioned the possibility of Leah's being pregnant. He didn't need to. It was there between them like a living, breathing monster. He hadn't made love to her, either. Leah didn't know if he ever intended to touch her again.

"What time is your doctor's appointment?" he asked as he poured himself a cup of coffee.

"Nine."

"I want you to call me."

"At the office?" Although she had the phone number for the newspaper, she'd never contacted him there before.

"Yes. I'll be in most of the morning."

Waiting for your call. He didn't say it, but they both knew he could have.

"All right," she said, keeping her back to him.

"I'll talk to you later."

Leah nodded. "Later."

It wasn't until the door closed that she realized he'd left for work. Without kissing her goodbye, without saying another word, he'd walked away.

Tears rained down her cheeks; there was no penting up her emotions any longer. She turned off the burner and brought the plate of french toast to the table where the boys were waiting.

She was grateful when the twins didn't seem to notice she was weeping. She let them dish up their own plates, spread the butter and pour the syrup—half of which ended up on the table.

Rubbing her eyes, she sat down with the boys, but, like Paul, she didn't have much of an appetite lately. Holding her coffee cup in her hands, she braced her elbows against the table.

"Leah?"

Ronnie stood beside her chair, his big blue eyes gazing up at her.

"What is it, sweetheart?"

"Here," he said, shoving his yellow blanket into her lap.

Touched by his generosity, Leah hugged him close. It was then that the sobs overtook her.

Paul had gone forty-eight hours on less than five hours' sleep. He'd woken feeling as though the two hours he'd slept had done him more harm than good. He would have been better off not going to bed at all than to wake as he did—feeling part zombie, part human.

Furthermore he was dangerous in this condition—to himself and to others. He was halfway to work before he realized he'd left the house. It wouldn't have concerned him so much if he hadn't been driving. He couldn't even remember leaving home or saying goodbye to Leah and the children. If he had, the memory had escaped him.

The phone rang on his desk, and Paul nearly tore the receiver off the cradle in his anxiety to answer it.

"Paul Manning."

"All right, what's going on?" It was Jason.

"What do you mean?"

"Between you and Leah. Dinner Saturday night was supposed to have been a celebration."

"It was..."

"Not from where I sat," Jason countered.

"Leave it," Paul said crisply. He wasn't one to share his problems and never had been. If Leah was pregnant, the news would come out soon enough. There wasn't any reason to air his troubles with Jason.

"Not this time, big brother."

"I don't have time to talk," Paul said crossly, "I'm expecting an important phone call."

"From whom?"

"Leah," Paul said without thinking.

"Do you expect her to phone and apologize?"

Paul laughed. "You aren't going to trick me into discussing my marital problems, so don't even try."

"I wasn't," Jason denied. "Damn it, Paul, would you stop being so almighty proud for once? We're family. You seem to think that just because you're the oldest you aren't supposed to have problems. Well, I've got news for you, big brother. You aren't any better than the rest of us."

"I never thought I was."

"Then tell me what's wrong with you and Leah. I can't remember when I've seen any two people look more unhappy."

Paul hesitated and wiped his hand down his face. He was weary in body and spirit. Worried sick. Frightened out of his wits, and he didn't know what he was going to do. Make a counseling appointment, spill his guts to a professional. He felt as though that was what he needed. Experienced help.

He sighed and pinched the bridge of his nose. "Leah thinks she might be pregnant," he admitted hoarsely.

"Dear God."

"My sentiments exactly," Paul said, grateful his brother understood his fear. Grateful, too, Jason hadn't made some stupid comment about wondering when Paul was going to learn to keep his pants zipped. They were zipped now. He hadn't touched Leah in two nights, which was like closing the barn door after the horse had escaped. It hadn't eased his mind, either. If anything, it had multiplied tenfold the tension between them.

"When is she going to the doctor?"

"This morning. She said she'd phone once she was home."

"How does she feel about it?"

Paul had to stop and think. The hell if he knew. He'd never stopped to ask her. "I . . . don't know," he admitted reluctantly.

"What about you?"

"Dear God, Jason, I've never been so frightened in my life. I haven't slept in two nights . . . the thought of losing Leah . . ."

"You won't."

"How can you be so damn sure?" he demanded. "Diane had given birth to twins without much of a problem. Who would have believed a second pregnancy would kill her?"

"I understand your fears."

"You couldn't possibly know what I'm going through."

"Perhaps not, but aren't you forgetting something?"

"What?" Paul demanded impatiently.

"Leah."

"Yes, but . . ." Paul stopped cold. Jason was right. He'd been so wrapped up in his own fears that he hadn't taken Leah's feelings into consideration. Not even once. If she showed any fear of being pregnant, he hadn't sensed it in her. Dear, sweet heaven, he didn't know how she could not be afraid. He was terrified, and they weren't even certain yet.

"But what?" Jason prompted.

"She doesn't seem to be overly frightened at the prospect of being pregnant." If anything, Paul had detected a hint of exhilaration, a joyful expectation. He hadn't dwelled on it, not with his fears running rampant. Not with the guilt beating him down like a garbage compactor. Fear, regret and anxiety had been his closest friends of late.

"In other words all Leah knows is that you're scared."

"No." It wasn't until he was talking to his brother that Paul realized how badly he'd bungled things. "All she knows is that I'm angry."

"Angry."

"Yes, damn it, angry."

"With her?"

"No," he said forcefully. "That wouldn't make the least bit of sense. I'm furious with myself."

"And she knows this?"

"Of course she knows it." He assumed she knew it. Assumed she realized his concern was for her, because he loved her so much. Because his life revolved around her.

"You're sure of this?"

Paul rubbed his hand along the back of his neck. "You know, Jason, you've missed your calling in life. You should work as a police interrogator."

Jason chuckled and for the first time in what seemed like an eternity, Paul smiled, too. "I can see there're some fences I need to mend with my wife. I suppose I should thank you for being so kind as to point them out to me."

"Any time. If I ever marry, which isn't likely, you can bet you'll be the one I turn to in times of trouble."

"Frankly," Paul said unevenly, "I don't think that would be such a good idea."

"Why not?"

"Because I've got to be about the worst example of a husband you could find."

"Don't be so hard on yourself. You're only human."

"Would you care to explain that to Leah for me?"

"Not on your life. That, big brother, is something only you can do."

"That's what I thought you'd say."

It wasn't easy, but with a little begging and a lot of hard bargaining, Paul managed to get what remained of the day off. What he had to say to Leah couldn't be said over the phone, nor could it wait. He'd been a selfish fool, so wrapped up in himself and his own fears that he'd managed to hurt the one person in the world he'd give anything not to.

He drove directly home, parked in the driveway and leapt out of the car. He raced into the kitchen to find Leah folding a load of diapers. He stopped abruptly.

"I ... I tried to phone the office twice," she said quietly, her voice low and weak. "They said you weren't there. I left a message."

Now that he was home, facing his wife, Paul found himself at a loss for words. He held his arms out to her.

"I did try to phone," she said again. "There wasn't any reason for you to rush home."

"Stop, don't say anything more."

She looked at him as though she wasn't sure she knew what to expect. He folded her in his arms, cherishing the warm feel of her, drinking in her softness.

Cupping her face between his hands, he gazed down on her face. The sight of her puffy eyes convinced him she'd been crying. It broke his heart to realize he was the source of her unhappiness.

"Leah," he said, then paused, not knowing how to proceed. Showing her how he felt seemed much easier. He loved her and it was high time she knew it. He kissed her hungrily, deeply, his mouth moving over hers with a gentle savagery, with a desperation that bordered on wild. "I love you, Leah," he chanted. "I love you so damn much."

"Paul...I'm not..." She tried to break away from him, and he felt the resistance in her, felt the restraint shudder through her body. He knew he'd won whatever battle she was waging within herself when she parted her lips to him and their tongues met.

Leah broke away and buried her face in his chest, her shoulders heaving. "Why tell me that now?" she asked in a voice that both demanded and begged.

"Because it's true...because I should have told you long before. I've been worried sick you might be pregnant and..."

"I'm not."

"You're not?"

"The doctor said he doesn't know why my period's so late. It probably has something to do with anxiety, but I can't recall being upset about anything."

The relief that washed over Paul felt like water on a parched garden. He tried not to show it, not to show how grateful he was not to have to face this fear head-on so soon after they'd been married. So soon after he'd found happiness again.

"You'll be happy to hear something else."

"What's that?"

"I'm not likely to get pregnant, either . . . I'm starting on birth control pills, so you won't need to worry about me bearing you a child you don't want."

Chapter Eleven

"It isn't that I don't want another child," Paul started to explain, but Leah turned away, not wanting to hear him. She reached for a diaper and held it protectively against her stomach.

"Paul, I know what your feelings were. Please don't try to sugarcoat them now. You could barely look at me.... You haven't touched me since...Friday night. This morning you left for work without even bothering to say goodbye...as though you couldn't wait to get away from me."

"Leah, it's not what you think." His hands settled on her shoulders, but when she stiffened he released her. He walked around the table so she wouldn't have any choice but to look at him, although she still avoided eye contact.

"What else was there for me to think?" she asked with as much dignity as she could muster. "That you'd be overjoyed if I was pregnant? Did you lead me to believe you'd arrange for someone to take the children so we could celebrate alone? Did you arrive home with a quart of my favorite ice cream and a jar of dill pickles?"

Her words had the desired affect. He went pale. It was how Diane and Paul had celebrated when they'd learned Diane was pregnant with Kelsey. Alone, their happiness bubbling over, their love and excitement centered around one another.

"I got the message, Paul. Loud and clear."

"It's just that I was so afraid of losing you."

"Exactly. Who'd be here to wash and clean for you? Who'd be here to raise your children and most important of all... who'd satisfy you sexually? You'd miss me all right, but for all the wrong reasons."

"Leah... no. It isn't like that. I love you."

"I saw how much you love me." She tossed the diaper down on the table and walked into the backyard. Her garden was in full bloom now, the tomato plants heavy with reddening fruit. A fresh load of laundry, the sheets from the twins' beds, flapped in the wind.

She stood with her back to the house and brushed the tears from her eyes. A soft sound coming from behind alerted her that Paul had followed her outside.

"I may have cheated you in a lot of ways," he admitted, his words low and deceptively soft. "You didn't have the courtship you deserved or even the wedding you should have had. There are probably countless other ways in which you've been slighted in this marriage. But I never intended it to be like this—I never meant to be so thoughtless and self-centered.

"But not the sex, Leah. Not the sex. That's been something beautiful we've shared together. Something we discovered on our own, in our own time. You can fault me in every other area, but not that one. There, I've given as much as I took."

"You're right," she answered, rubbing the tears from her face. "We have a marvelous sex life. I can't argue that point, can I? I . . . I've wanted you, too."

A long moment passed. "I love you, Leah. I know you don't believe me. I can't blame you if you don't believe me, but it's the truth." The words fell between them, filled with pain and regret. "What can I do?"

"Do?"

"To right the wrongs . . . to prove to you I mean what I say. To make up to you for the way I acted when I thought you might be pregnant."

Leah didn't know. Even if it were possible, there was nothing she would change. She had moved into his home voluntarily. Married him of her own free will. She loved the children, loved being their mother, and, God help her, she loved Paul, too. With all her heart and soul, she loved Paul.

"Tell me, and whatever it is you want me to do, I'll do it."

"It's not that simple."

"I know."

She turned to face him then, her heart hammering like a boxer's fist against a punching bag. When she went to speak, her mouth opened but the words refused to come out. "Just . . ."

"Yes." He moved one step closer to her. One small step.

"Just . . . love me . . ."

"I do. Dear God, Leah, I do." He reached for her then, burying his face in the curve of her shoulder, his body shuddering against hers.

". . . the same way you loved Diane."

"How does it feel to have the boys in school half days?" Jamie Manning asked Leah three days later. The two were shopping in the mall, pushing their strollers side by side down the concourse and checking out the sales.

"They love it."

"What about you?"

"The truth?" Leah said, smiling toward her sister-in-law. "I love it, too."

"Free at last," Jamie cried dramatically, then, glancing down at Kelsey, amended the statement. "Well, almost free."

"I can't believe how much more time I seem to have with the boys gone mornings. Wait until Bethany starts preschool and you'll know what I mean."

Jamie paused as they neared the area where several fast-food outlets were situated. "Do you think we dare stay for an early lunch?"

Leah checked her watch. "How brave do you feel?"

"I've always been pretty daring."

"Kelsey likes to toss her food."

"No problem, we'll sit as far away from other people as possible."

Leah was game. It felt good to get out of the house for a while, although shopping had never excited her much before. Now that there were Paul and the children to buy for, she enjoyed finding bargains.

Taking a morning off to spend with Jamie had lifted her spirits. The past couple of weeks had been strained between her and Paul. He was trying, with everything in him he was trying, but instead of helping, it had only made matters worse. The harder he tried to prove his love for her, the more forced it seemed. Paul was in a no-win situation, and Leah had placed him there.

Leah needed a confidante. A friend. Jamie, either by design or luck, was fast becoming both.

Leah bought herself a chicken salad and Kelsey an order of french fries. Jamie ordered a slice of pizza for herself and bread sticks for Bethany. Within a few minutes they had the toddlers set up in the high chairs the mall provided and were sitting at a small white table as far away from the other diners as they could get.

"By the way," Jamie said, looking at Leah's wrist, "is that a new watch?"

She nodded, swallowing a bite of her salad. "Paul got it for me. I happened to mention how much I like Mickey Mouse and the very next day he brought home this."

"Your birthday?"

"No." Leah set aside her plastic fork and lowered her head. "He . . . he feels guilty."

"Guilty? Why?"

She shrugged, not sure she should continue. "We . . . thought I was pregnant not long ago. Paul doesn't want another baby. I realize a lot of what he was feeling had to do with what happened to my sister, but at the same time I was terribly hurt by the way he acted."

Jamie set her pizza aside and nodded. "We have a lot in common, Leah, more than you realize. Rich and I didn't come into our marriage in the typical way, either. In fact we made the arrangements for a divorce at the same time we planned the wedding."

Leah knew the gist of Jamie and Rich's marriage story, but not the details. "You married Rich because you wanted a baby?"

Jamie smiled and smoothed the soft blond curls from her daughter's forehead. "It was something like that. I wanted a baby all right, mainly because I didn't ever intend to marry. I wanted Rich to be the father. It made sense at the time to approach him, since I wasn't in love with him. Oh, I mean, I was in love with him, only I didn't realize it at the time. I told myself he should be Bethany's father because he had the right genetic makeup." She paused and laughed. "We both know what a handsome cuss Rich is. We'd been friends since high school and I approached him on that basis. Friend to friend. I wanted him to be my baby's sperm donor."

"And he agreed to this?" It didn't sound anything like the Rich Leah knew.

"He insisted, for a variety of reasons, that we marry. I wasn't keen on the idea, but I went along with it because I knew it was the only way Rich would agree to my plan."

"Then Bethany was conceived, artificially?"

Jamie laughed once more. "No, she was conceived the good old-fashioned way. The same way this baby was." She flattened her hand against her abdomen and gently patted her tummy. "So you see, I didn't come into this family as a traditional bride, either."

"I imagine you and Rich thought Paul was crazy to marry me the way he did."

"No," Jamie said thoughtfully after a moment. "The circumstances were unusual, but ours weren't any less so. You've been so good for Paul, good for the children, too." She hesitated once more. "Do you love him?"

"Yes." All of Leah's heart went into the lone word.

"I knew you did. He loves you, too."

Leah dropped her gaze. She wasn't nearly as confident of Paul's feelings as she was her own. He needed her, for a hundred different reasons. But she would always be left wondering if he truly loved her. For herself. For Leah, the intelligent, plain Baker sister.

When he had told her he loved her that morning two weeks earlier, it had seemed like a miracle. She realized now it was the only thing he could say under the circumstances, knowing how badly he'd hurt her. He was seeking a way to atone for the pain he'd unwittingly inflicted. Leah wanted to believe him so badly. He had touched a chord in her she hadn't known existed, satisfied a craving that reached far back into her childhood. In all her life, no man had ever really loved her. Not her father, who had abandoned her when she was barely old enough to remember him. Not her mother, either. Leah had never been able to satisfy her mother. Over the years she'd dated some, but not much. Just enough for her to know that whatever it was a woman possessed to make a man happy, Leah Baker lacked.

Until Paul. He made her vulnerable in ways she'd never know she could be. Vulnerable to love. Vulnerable to a happiness she'd never expected to find. Vulnerable to a gentleness, a tenderness that touched her heart.

"He's trying so hard," Leah whispered. Trying to give her all the things she'd missed before their marriage. In the past two weeks he'd brought her gifts, complimented her for just about everything, wooed her back into his bed and loved her with an urgency that melted any resistance she tried to harbor.

He was trying so hard . . . to love her, for herself.

"Rich and I experienced our own set of problems," Jamie went on to say. "We never intended for there to be anything physical between us. It was supposed to have been a marriage of convenience, but it turned out to be one of inconvenience."

"What happened?"

Jamie took a sip of her soft drink before answering. "I made the silly mistake of having dinner with a former boyfriend. It wasn't a date, wasn't even close to one. He was married and having problems and needing someone to listen to him."

"Rich was jealous?"

"Terribly. But to be fair to Rich, his feelings were understandable. The woman he'd recently broken up with had been two-timing him—it seemed to Rich that I was doing the same thing. Everything blew up in our faces."

"But it smoothed out in time?"

"Eventually, but matters got worse before they got better."

Leah understood that all too well. "It seems to work that way in most cases, doesn't it?"

Jamie's hand tightened around her soft drink. "I guess what I'm trying to say is, I don't want you to be discouraged. I've known Paul for a good many years. He's an honorable man. I can't believe he would ever have married you if he didn't truly love you. If you're experiencing problems now, don't worry about it, all couples do. There's a period of adjustment for all newlyweds." Jamie hesitated. "I sound like I really know what I'm talking about, don't I?"

Leah smiled. "I appreciate hearing it, but even more than that I appreciate having someone I can talk to.... I miss Diane so much...I not only lost my sister—I lost my best friend."

"Paul understands that," Jamie said quietly. "Diane was his best friend, too."

It was Friday night. Late Friday night. Leah sat up in bed reading, and Paul was working feverishly in his den, writing the last chapter of his novel. A marathon session. Leah decided she'd wait for him, which wasn't much of a problem since she was deeply involved in a whodunit by one of her favorite authors.

Closing her book, Leah climbed out of bed and walked into the kitchen, searching out a snack. Something other than graham crackers and peanut butter. She was bent over the lower shelf of the refrigerator when Paul spoke from behind her.

"Now that's an inviting pose if I ever saw one."

"Paul," she chided, straightening, clenching a chicken leg in her hand. She closed the refrigerator door and turned around. "Are you finished?"

He nodded.

"Are you going to let me read it?"

He crossed his arms and leaned against the door frame, smiling indolently, proudly. "That depends."

"On what?" she asked suspiciously, her eyes narrowing.

"On how much you appreciate literary genius."

"Oh, I appreciate genius, all right." Paul seemed more relaxed than she'd seen him in weeks. It felt good to banter with him, to joke and smile.

"Might I suggest you toss that chicken leg, woman?" He held his arms out to her.

Leah gave up her snack to move willingly into his embrace.

His arms fit around her waist as he lifted her from the floor. "It's taken me nearly two years to get this book on paper."

"But you did it, Paul, you did it."

"I believe a reward would be fitting, don't you?" His gaze focused on her lips.

"What kind of reward?"

His eyes darkened in unspoken invitation. "I have a feeling you'll think of something."

"I'm thinking, all right."

He fit his hands intimately over her buttocks, lifting her upward so her abdomen rested squarely against his sex. "Are you thinking the same thing I'm thinking?" He wiggled his eyebrows suggestively.

"Paul Manning, you shock me."

"All I'm asking for is a few kisses."

"Oh, right. I'm supposed to believe you'll be satisfied with that?"

"It's a start." His mouth greedily sought hers, and Leah greedily offered him what he wanted.

They kissed again, with a hunger that scorched her senses. When next she looked up, they were in the bedroom and Paul was getting ready to place her on the mattress. Their eyes met. His, blue and serious—blue and passionate—the teasing laughter faded.

"It's been a week, Leah."

"Five days, but who's counting?"

"I have been," he countered impatiently. "It's been hell."

She didn't understand. Paul hadn't made love to her in five days, but he'd been loving and gentle and concerned. She hadn't thought he'd been holding back; she'd assumed he'd just been tired or preoccupied.

"Have you wanted to make love to me before now?" she asked as he hurriedly unfastened the buttons of his shirt.

"Yes."

"Then why didn't you?"

"Do you have to be quite so talkative just this minute?" He sat on the bed and jerked off his shoes.

"Paul, I'm serious." Uncertain, she stood.

His arms reached for her, gripping her about the waist. "Baby, so am I." His hands caught the hem of her gown, peeling it from her head, then he captured her about the waist and brought her closer to him. She stood between his spread legs while he remained seated on the bed.

"Paul, we should talk about this. I had no idea..."

"In a minute." He placed his hands over the rounded crest of her buttocks and drew her closer to him, until his mouth could catch the extended point of her nipples. He kissed them in turn, paying attention to each breast, feasting on her, applying a sweet suckling pressure until Leah moaned and buried her hands in his hair, holding him against her.

When he finished, he nuzzled her breasts with his nose. "Still want me to answer those questions?"

"Ah..."

"That's what I thought." His hands lifted her breasts, bunched them together while his thumbs caressed the undersides. "Have I told you lately how much I want you?" he asked as he buried his face in her bounty.

"No...you haven't showed me, either."

"That, my dear wife, is about to be remedied." He released her reluctantly, stood and unzipped his pants.

Leah triumphantly noticed, long before he stepped out of his clothing, the rigid line of his manhood. He positioned himself over her, his eyes holding hers.

Leah smiled softly and reached up to him. Paul made a small noise as he thrust deep into the hot folds of her womanhood.

Leah sighed with pleasure. She'd never known anything so keen or so good. He began to move, slowly at the beginning, and then gradually accelerating his thrusts until he'd brought her to the brink of a bold new universe where they were hurled together into a black hole, an unfathomable sphere, their arms entwined around one another.

Paul stared into the night, his arms fixed about his wife, feeling utterly content, utterly satisfied. They had made love for hours, yet the physical completion had come within minutes of entering the bedroom. He was so eager for her, so needy. Unable to restrain himself, he'd had her flat on her back, her legs hugging his waist, and was buried as deeply as he could in her incredible warmth.

The urgency he felt to make love to Leah hadn't changed in the weeks since their marriage. He didn't understand it even now, but he'd given up questioning his need for her. It was just there. Potent and powerful.

He'd worked harder these past couple of weeks at controlling it, for fear she'd accuse him of using her sexually. Maybe on some deep, psychological level he feared it himself. So he was rationing himself. Once a week—that was all the sex he'd decided to allot himself.

Maybe twice, he amended; there wasn't any need to be stingy. No need to raise Leah's concern should she notice. Yes, twice a week made far more sense. Wednesdays and Saturdays. Maybe Monday and Thursdays and either Saturday or Sunday. No, that was three times a week.

Oh, what the hell, three times a week shouldn't tax her too much. Should it?

He smiled to himself as she nestled her head against his chest. He hadn't slept yet, and it would soon be morning. Close to the time the twins and Kelsey would wake.

He didn't care how much sleep he'd lost; this night had been worth every second of wasted slumber. The last time he'd looked at the clock it had been past four. Leah had retrieved her chicken leg and brought it into bed, claiming she was hungry. Who wouldn't be after the work-out they'd just completed?

She couldn't let her appetite go unattended, she had said, attacking the leg. A college professor—even one taking a leave of absence—couldn't live on love alone.

She was sheer joy. Dear, sweet heaven, how he loved her.

His book was finished. After two long years he finally had the story down. There'd been a sense of fulfillment, an overwhelming sensation of accomplishment and pride, printing out the last chapter. He would read it over in the morning, do what editing needed to be done and then mail it, lock, stock and barrel, off to New York. Then the waiting game would begin.

Paul was beginning to feel a cautious optimism about life. He was happy. Not close to being happy. Just plain happy. Once he realized that, he paused, wondering if he should be feeling that way. No, he decided. He wasn't going to censure himself. He wasn't going to examine his joy under a microscope and punish himself for feeling alive.

He had loved Diane. Loved her even now. She'd been his first real love, his first wife, the mother of his children. But she was in the past. His yesterday. In many ways she would always be a part of him. But she was gone.

In her stead he'd found Leah. She was his heart now. His soul. His joy.

After bungling the first few weeks of their marriage, he'd done everything he could think of to make it up to her, to show her how much he cared. In his own way, on a limited budget, with limited time, he'd been courting her.

Leah was now the one who'd brought happiness back into his life. He could laugh now. The grief that had weighted him down for so many months had left him. The shadow of it didn't follow him or haunt him any longer. It just disappeared one day; he didn't know when, hadn't even realized it. He'd just looked up and it was gone, disappeared.

He was free. Free to laugh. Free to appreciate life. All his senses were fine-tuned. More poignant. More intense than ever before.

It was as if he'd woken up one morning and found himself alive after giving himself up for dead for so long. When had it happened? Paul didn't know, but he was sure he'd recognized its beginning.

It had started when Leah had decided to move in with him and the children. His whole world had taken a one-hundred-and-eighty-degree turn for the better that day.

They'd had their problems, but then all couples did. Leah was trying to make their marriage work, too. Slowly she was lowering the self-imposed walls as he gained her trust, as he won her confidence bit by bit.

Leah wasn't Diane. She was more sensitive. Less open. A little more guarded, but he was learning. He was learning.

His eyes drifted closed. He was ready to sleep.

He dreamed of her that night.

Diane.

He'd fallen into a deep sleep, happy and content, and woke with a sick feeling in the pit of his stomach. A feeling of deep loss and sorrow. A sense of regret. A feeling he'd thought was gone forever.

Try as he might, Paul couldn't remember the details of the dream, only that it had involved Diane. He sat up in bed and held his head between his hands as though nursing a world-class hangover.

How could this have happened? Now? It made no sense. He'd set everything to order in his mind. Lined all his ducks up in a tidy row. Made his soul-wrenching resolutions and chosen life. Chosen love.

Leah was awake. He could hear her in the kitchen with the children. He staggered out of bed and abruptly dressed.

Kelsey was sitting in her high chair waving a spoon. The boys were stationed in front of the television set watching Saturday-morning cartoons. Leah was standing in front of the kitchen sink, sipping from a cup of coffee.

"Morning," he said, wiping a hand down his face. "You should have woken me."

Leah didn't answer.

"Leah?" He reached for a mug and poured himself a cup of coffee.

She kept her back to him still.

"Is something wrong?"

She shook her head and set aside her coffee before walking down the hallway to the bedroom.

He took a minute to drink down some coffee, unclog his mind, before he followed her. She was sitting on the end of the bed, looking lost and small and vulnerable.

He sat next to her, his stomach twisted in tight knots, dread filling the inside of his mouth. "What happened?"

"Nothing."

"Leah, for the love of heaven, don't play games with me. Obviously something's upset you. Tell me what it is."

She was holding a tissue in her hand and had wound it around her index finger several times. "You . . . were asleep."

"The dream." It came to him with sudden clarity. "Did I call you Diane?"

Leah nodded.

"I...I had a dream. I don't know why, I just did. She was in it. I'm sorry, Leah, sorrier than you know, but I swear to you by everything I hold dear that I didn't do it intentionally."

"I know that."

"All I can do is ask you to forgive me, although God knows it wasn't anything I planned."

"It isn't you who needs to be forgiven."

Paul closed his eyes, weary to the bone. "What do you want me to do, get down on my knees and beg you to forgive me?"

"No."

"Then what? Tell me."

"I can't kid myself any longer, Paul."

"Kid yourself?"

"Diane was my sister, I loved her...she was my best friend. From the time we were children, even though she was younger, she was better than me in every area except grades. She was bright and pretty and fun. I was dull and boring and plain."

"Leah, for the love of heaven . . ."

"No, let me finish. Please, let me finish while I have the courage. I never competed with her, never allowed myself to be put in that position, because I knew, I always knew I'd be the loser. The problem isn't you, Paul, it's me."

"I don't understand."

"I've discovered I'm greedy and jealous and I hate myself for it. I hate thinking the things I do. I hate feeling sick with envy because you love Diane. I feel guilty and miserable and I don't know that I can go on like this any longer."

"Leah, Diane's gone. I've let her go—released her. She's my past. You're my present, my future."

"I wish it were that simple," she said, swallowing back a sob.

"You don't need to compete with her."

Leah turned to look at him, her gaze unflinching. "Do you love her?"

He didn't hesitate. "Yes, but I love you, too."

"I need some time...to think, to sort out my feelings. I'm sorry, terribly sorry."

"Time?" Dear, sweet God, she was going to leave him. His heart was in turmoil, his head spinning. Could he have found happiness only to lose it once again?

"I...can't sleep with you anymore, Paul. You want me, you desire me, but it's Diane you love. It's Diane you call for in the dead of night. Not me. For the first time in my life I'm not willing to take second place to my sister. For once, just this once, I want something just for me, to be loved just for me."

She started to cry then, and Paul knew there was nothing he could say that would comfort her.

Chapter Twelve

Paul drove around for several hours in an effort to clear his head. He parked his car when he found himself outside the small apartment complex his brother Jason owned. He sat there for several minutes wondering if he should talk to his younger brother.

He hadn't made a habit of discussing his problems with anyone, not even family. Generally he preferred to work matters out in his own way, without collecting the counsel of relations or friends.

But Jason had said something recently that had struck a strong chord with Paul. His brother had said it was high time Paul realized he wasn't any better than the rest of them . . . that he should quit being so damn arrogant.

His brother's assessment of him had taken Paul by surprise. Jason and Rich viewed him as pompous! Hell, and he thought he was being strong.

Not dragging out his troubles for others to dissect wasn't a matter of pride, Paul had reasoned at the time. He was the eldest in a family of five children. The others looked up to him. He was their role model. He could almost hear his parents' words leaping out from his youth, reminding him of how important it was for him to be a good example to the others.

He'd gotten so accustomed to keeping his worries to himself that he wasn't sure he knew how to ask for help. Or even if he should.

After several minutes Paul climbed out of the car and walked toward Jason's apartment. He'd assumed Jason had made a foolish mistake buying the eight-unit complex. As far as he was concerned, renters were nothing but trouble. But his brother didn't seem to be having much of a problem. He managed the building himself, made sure he got the right tenants, then lay back and collected the rent money each month.

Jason answered the door, wearing a football jersey and a baseball cap. The second-oldest Manning had been a sports fanatic since they were kids. He'd been on the varsity cross-country, track and swim teams in high school, and he'd continued with cross-country in college.

These days all Jason played was softball, and the season had ended a couple of weeks earlier. But he still loved to watch any kind of sport.

"Paul." He sounded surprised to see him.

"Morning."

"It's afternoon."

Paul checked his watch and was surprised to find his brother was right. "So it is."

"Come on in. Notre Dame's just about to kick off." He motioned toward his sofa where a bag of potato chips had spilled across the coffee table and a can of soda was sitting on top of the morning paper.

Paul had only been to Jason's home one time before, shortly after his brother had bought the apartment building. A look around assured him Jason wasn't much of a housekeeper. A week's worth or more of newspapers was carelessly scattered across the beige carpet. A partial load of laundry, towels it looked like, was heaped up on the recliner. Several glasses and a variety of plates and eating utensils littered the living-room area.

Jason plopped himself down in front of the television. "Make yourself at home."

Paul sat down and for a time pretended to pay attention to the college football game.

"You want something to eat?"

"No, thanks," Paul said as he reached for a potato chip and munched on it before he realized what he was doing.

"So matters aren't working out between you and Leah?" Jason asked with that easygoing manner of his, as if his business was prying into other people's private affairs. If he hadn't so accurately detected his problem, Paul might have been insulted.

"How'd you know that?" He hated the fact that his younger brother could read him so well. Paul had always thought of himself as a cool cucumber, adept at disguising his emotions. Apparently he wasn't nearly as clever as he'd assumed.

"You got the look, big brother," Jason said, grinning.

"The look?" Paul frowned.

"Yeah, you look guilty as hell. What'd you do this time?"

"Why are you so sure it was me?" Paul argued.

"Because it generally is the man," Jason said without taking his eyes off the television screen.

"For not being married, you certainly seem to be an expert on this." Paul almost wished he'd gone to Rich and talked matters over with the youngest Manning brother. Paul knew Leah had been shopping with Jamie earlier in the week. He was pleased to hear it, delighted the two had become friends. If he was going to spill his guts, Rich was the more logical choice, yet it was Jason he found himself turning to for advice.

"You're right, you know. I am guilty as hell."

"You want to talk about it?"

Paul nodded and rubbed his palms together as he gathered his thoughts.

Jason reached for the television controller and turned off the set. "You want something to drink? Soda? Beer? Coffee?"

With so many other matters on his mind, Paul found making a decision almost impossible. "Coffee, I guess." He followed his brother into the kitchen and marveled that there were any clean dishes left in the house. Dirty pots and pans lined the sink and counter. The joys of living alone.

Jason opened the dishwasher, pulled out a mug and examined it first before filling it with tap water. He opened the microwave, removed a pair of socks and then set the mug inside.

While the water was heating, Paul paced the small kitchen. "I had a dream last night...about Diane." He paused, half expecting Jason to comment. When his brother didn't, he continued. "I don't remember anything about the dream . . . only that she was in it."

"Has this happened before?"

"Not that I remember." Paul had never been one to dream much. "I don't understand it. If Diane was going to haunt my sleep, why now? Why would she come back just when I've made my peace with her death? It doesn't make any sense to me."

Jason apparently didn't have any answers for him, either.

"I've remarried and for the first time in almost a year I can say I'm happy, truly at peace with myself. Leah and I are...were," he amended sadly, "working everything out. I've been doing my damnedest to be a good husband to her, to make up for the things I didn't do earlier. Now this."

"Don't go hitting yourself over the head because of a dream."

"It was more than that," Paul admitted sheepishly. "Last night, Leah and I—" he hesitated "—I don't know how to explain it. It was as though for the first time all the barriers were down between us. I'd finished my novel."

"Congratulations."

Paul smiled weakly. "Thanks." He wasn't nearly as excited as he had been. The project was finished, but the exhilaration was gone. Nothing was more important to him than his relationship with his wife.

"Leah and I made love and . . . I don't know how to describe it, Jase, it was so incredibly beautiful. I held her in my arms and it came to me how much my life had changed since I'd married her.

"I feel so whole again. This serenity was a long time coming. I realized I loved Diane and always will, but she's gone and I'm alive, and for the first time since I buried her, I'm not sorry to be."

"You've come a long way, Paul."

Paul wished he could believe that. "When I went to sleep I was at peace with myself and my world, and then I had to go and have the dream."

"Did it occur to you that maybe Diane was saying goodbye to you?" Jason asked softly.

"Saying goodbye to me... I don't understand."

"You just finished saying you'd fully accepted her death."

"Yes."

"Perhaps your subconscious allowed her the opportunity to release you, too. I remember after Kelsey was born there was only a short time before Diane went into the coma. There wasn't much of a chance for the two of you to talk, was there?"

"No. Not really. It happened so fast, within just a matter of days she was gone."

"I know." Jason's eyes were somber.

"I wish I remembered more of the dream," Paul protested, "but I don't."

"Is it important?"

Paul pulled out a kitchen chair and sat down. The burden of his guilt had never felt heavier. "There's more. I don't know how it happened, but at some point during the night I called Leah *Diane*."

Jason issued a low, tension-filled whistle and slowly shook his head. "Not a smart move, big brother."

"I didn't do it on purpose."

"Of course you didn't. Surely Leah understands that."

"I don't know what she's thinking. She was crying and, to be truthful, she wasn't making a whole lot of sense. She kept saying she couldn't compete with Diane anymore, and that she was moving out of our bedroom because I loved Diane. I'm not supposed to have loved her?" he demanded. "How am I supposed to stop loving her? She was my wife."

"Give Leah time. She's obviously upset, and when you think about it, you can't really blame her."

"As a matter of fact, I'm upset, too," Paul said heatedly. "Where does this put me? I'm supposed to tell Leah I don't love Diane anymore?"

"She wouldn't believe you even if you did."

"I know," Paul admitted, defeat weighing down his shoulders until he slumped forward. "I remember the day I married Diane. It seems like a hundred years ago now, a thousand lifetimes back. We stood before the minister, and I recall thinking I was going to love this woman all my life. And the amazing part is, I will continue to love her. I can't stop, no more than I can understand how it's possible to love two women so intensely."

"You love Leah too, then?"

Paul nodded. "I didn't go into marriage with Leah with the same rosy vision I did with Diane. It made sense to marry her. Mom and Dad pointed out several things neither one of us had thought to consider. I was attracted to her. I admired her and respected her, and she didn't seem to object. But I didn't love her then, not the way I did when I married Diane."

"But you do now. Surely that means something."

"Apparently not a hell of a lot," he answered vehemently. "I didn't know a man possessed the capacity to love two women so deeply. For a long time I struggled with that, thinking I was cheating one or the other by loving both." It was a moment of self-realization for Paul; talking out his feelings to his brother like this was helping him clear the cobwebs out of his head. Many of the feelings he was discussing, he hadn't even been aware of before.

Jason didn't say much, but pulled out the chair across from him and sat down.

"Leah and I didn't start our physical relationship right away," Paul continued, a bit chagrined to be discussing his sex life with his bachelor brother. "Neither of us were ready for it."

"At least you were wise enough to recognize as much. Not everyone would have."

"For a while I was convinced I was being unfaithful to Diane's memory by loving Leah. But try as I might, I couldn't make myself not love her."

"She's your wife, it only makes sense that you feel the way you do."

In his heart Paul knew Leah was just as miserable as he was. He had tried to talk to her that morning, tried to reason with her, but she was beyond the point of listening. Not knowing what more to say or do, Paul had silently slipped out of the house.

He'd felt numb as he drove around. Numbness frightened him. For the first few days after Diane's death he'd experienced an anesthetized sensation. Gradually a red-hot emotional pain had overtaken him, and the grief had dominated every waking moment.

The agony had been so keen that his mind had blotted out whole weeks of time. He had functioned, he had gone to work, he had taken care of his children, lived day to day as best he could, but he didn't remember much of what had happened.

It had all started with a numbness then, the same numbness he'd felt that morning when Leah told him he'd called her by her sister's name.

"What are you going to do?" Jason asked him.

Paul had to pull his thoughts together, mull over his dilemma. "I don't know," he answered honestly. "Start rebuilding the trust with her as best I can. I'll love her without making any demands on her, give her the space and time she needs."

"That sounds like a good place to start."

Paul smiled. He never did get the cup of coffee his brother had promised him, but it didn't make any difference now. He was finished, or rather he had found a place to start.

"How'd you get so smart?" he asked Jason.

His brother lifted up his baseball cap and scratched the crown of his head. "I don't know, guess it just runs in the family."

Eager now to get back to Leah, Paul left his brother's place. He felt worlds better. Anxious to talk to her, to explain as best he could everything that had come out when he was talking to Jason.

More than anything, he longed to take her in his arms, hold her tight and fast and tell her how much he loved her, how much he needed her and how much he wanted her.

He pulled the car into the driveway and nearly leapt out, impatient to talk to his wife.

"Leah." Her name was on his lips even before he entered the front door.

He was met with silence. Taking giant steps, he walked into the kitchen to find Kelsey standing up and holding on to the seat of the chair. She gave him a four-tooth smile and wildly thrashed her arm about with excitement.

The neighborhood girl, Angie somebody—for the life of him Paul couldn't remember her last name—was slicing a banana at the counter.

"Oh, hi," she said, smiling broadly.

"Where's Leah?"

"She left about an hour ago."

"Did she say where she was going?"

"No. I'm sorry, I didn't think to ask. She gave me the phone number to..." She paused and reached for a slip of paper. "Here it is, Jamie and Rich's."

"Yes?" Paul prompted.

"She wasn't sure when you'd be back, so she said I should call Jamie if you weren't here before dinner-time. Apparently Jamie was going to come over and pick up the kids."

Paul's heart was pounding. "Did she tell you when she planned on coming back?"

Once again Angie shook her head. "I don't think it's any time soon. She must have been going on a trip or something because she had a suitcase with her."

Leah had no business being behind the wheel of a car and she knew it. Tears continued to stream down from her eyes, blurring her vision, making her driving a hazard to her and to others.

At a red light she paused and blew her nose, then ran the back of her hand across her eyes.

She didn't know where she was going, only that she had to get away. The logical thing to do was to check into a hotel room and shuffle through her emotions, try to make some sense of why she'd said the things she had to Paul. She needed to understand what was happening between her and Paul. Between her and Diane.

Finding somewhere to spend the night might have been the rational thing to do, but Leah was in no frame of mind to be rational. If she had been, she would never have done anything as stupid as packing her bag and walking out on Paul and the children.

He'd left her, without a word. He'd slipped out of the house, and she'd been alone to face the pain. To face the doubts and the fears. Everything seemed to crowd in on her, and she had felt the overwhelming need to get away.

Leah hated what was happening to her. What was happening to Paul. She'd reacted in anger, lashing back at him for the pain he had caused her. The same pain she'd carried with her most of her life, standing on the sidelines while her mother petted and fawned over Diane. She'd smiled and swallowed back the hurt when it was Diane who received new clothes at the beginning of the school year while Leah was given hand-me-downs from neighbors and friends.

She'd carried the hurt with her all those years, and yet she loved her sister. Diane couldn't be blamed for being pretty and sweet, any more than Leah could for being plain and bookwormish.

Then Diane had died and, ironic as it seemed, for the first time in her life Leah had a chance at finding happiness. She'd jealously guarded her heart for so many years. Protected herself from being vulnerable in relationships. If she was going to fall in love, why, dear God, why did it have to be with her dead sister's husband?

Paul had adored Diane. He adored her still. It didn't seem fair that the only man Leah had ever loved had to be a man who loved her sister so desperately.

They were so different. Leah and Diane. Leah could never hope to gain Paul's devotion. He loved her, Leah realized that, but what he felt for her paled in comparison to the depth of his love for Diane.

Once again, for the umpteenth time in her life, she was forced to stand in the shadow of her sister's limelight.

Leah had always been the reserved and quiet one. Diane had been sunshine and laughter. But for a while...for a short while Leah had learned how to laugh, too. The children had taught her. Paul had taught her.

Diane had died, and in her sister's stead, Leah had found everything her life had lacked. Abundant love. Acceptance. Joy and fulfillment. She'd found all those things, yet it wasn't enough.

She was jealous, but why now, when she'd never been jealous before? Early in life she'd accepted her lot, understood her place. So why now? Why after Diane was gone was Leah battling these feelings? It was irrational. Unfair.

Leah continued driving, taking side streets and staying off the busy thoroughfares. Her route led her past a golf course with rolling green hills. Golfers carrying umbrellas ambled from one green to another.

It came to her then. With a surprising jolt. She needed to talk to Diane, and even if it was a one-sided conversation, Leah had things that needed to be said.

Not knowing what street she was on, it took her some time to locate the cemetery. She parked and walked across the manicured lawn.

Nearly a year had passed since Diane's death. In all that time Leah hadn't once visited her sister's plot. She had stood at the grave site during the funeral—her heart breaking, her breath coming in tortured gasps—and had no desire to ever return.

Paul came often, or he had in the beginning. For months he'd brought fresh flowers out each and every week. Leah knew because she often watched the children while he was gone. Sometimes he'd be away for hours; other times it would be only a short while.

Leah couldn't recall when had been the last time. If he still came as often, he didn't mention it to her.

Wandering around, ignoring the drizzle, it took Leah almost an hour to find her sister's marker.

Diane Sandra Manning, Wife, Mother. The dates of her birth and death were listed along with a Scripture verse. It said so little.

It said so much.

She stood and looked down at the headstone. An overwhelming sense of sadness came at her in swells. Fresh tears filled her eyes, and she covered her mouth with her hand.

It took her several minutes to compose herself enough to speak. "Hi, Sis," she said when she could, her voice tight. "I bet you're surprised I came to see you."

It was foolish talking to a patch of lawn. In her heart Leah knew Diane wasn't there; she knew her sister would never hear the words she spoke. But none of that mattered to Leah.

"The boys started kindergarten classes. Oh, Diane, you'd be so proud of them. They're growing up so fast. Ryan came home from class last week proud as could be and announced anyone who could read five whole words didn't need a blankie. He gave it to me and hasn't asked for it back even once. Ronnie's given up his thumb, too." She smiled proudly as she smeared the tears across her cheek.

She hesitated and then started in again. "Kelsey's such a precious baby. She's walking now. Three and four steps at a time—she's so eager to get into everything. She's drinking out of a cup, too, but she still has two bottles a day." Leah folded her arms around her waist. "She has your coloring, her hair's so blond it's white. She's a beautiful little girl."

Leah opened her purse and took out a fresh tissue and wadded it up in her hand. "Paul finished his novel the other night," she said haltingly.

Then, squaring her shoulders, she closed her eyes. "I love him, too," she cried. "Is that what you wanted . . . for me to love Paul? I didn't mean for it to happen. . . . I'm not even sure when it did. One morning I woke up and realized it was too late . . . and I loved him.

"What am I supposed to do, Diane? I can't fight you for him. We can't sit down and talk this out the way we did when we were kids. You aren't going to hug me and reassure me. Paul is your husband. But now he's my husband, too. Is this what you intended? Is this what you wanted? For me to raise your children and to love Paul?'' She was sobbing so hard now, she could barely speak. "Because . . . that's what's happened and I feel so wretched."

Suddenly, unexpectedly, it stopped misting. The heavy dark clouds that had blanketed the sky most of the day parted, and a dazzling display of golden sunlight broke through, hitting the grass, causing it to glisten.

Leah looked toward the sky, feeling the sun's warmth seep into her bones.

Paul attempted to keep the panic out of his heart as he dialed his brother's phone number. It would be a bit more of a trick to keep the panic out of his voice.

"Hello."

Paul silently thanked the powers that be—it was his sister-in-law who picked up the phone. "Jamie, it's Paul," he said, managing to keep his voice conversationally smooth. "I just got home. I don't suppose you've heard from Leah?"

"Oh, hi, Paul. No, I can't say that I have. At least not since she phoned this morning."

"Did she happen to mention where she was going?"

Jamie didn't hesitate. Paul was listening, waiting for the slightest pause, hoping he wouldn't detect one so he'd know she was telling him the truth.

"No, she didn't. Is everything all right? You sound concerned."

"Everything's fine," he answered abruptly, far more interested in getting the information he needed than in giving reassurances, especially when they were in such short supply. "How did she sound when she talked to you?"

"About the same way you're sounding now. You're sure everything's all right?"

"Yes. What did she say?" he asked again.

"Not much, she phoned to ask if I could take the twins and Kelsey for her if you didn't get back before dinnertime. I told her it wouldn't be a problem."

"There wasn't anything more?" Paul was beyond the point of disguising his distress. Jamie didn't need him to spell out that he and Leah were having problems.

This time Jamie did hesitate. "It wasn't anything she said, exactly...."

"Yes?" he prompted.

"She sounded terribly upset, Paul, as though she'd been crying. But when I asked her about it, she tried to laugh. But her laugh sounded a whole lot more like a sob."

Paul felt wretched. He should never have left her. If he needed time alone, he could have mowed the lawn, sorted through his thoughts that way. "You're sure she didn't give you any indication of where she was going?"

"I'm sorry, Paul, but she didn't say. I don't think she knew herself."

That made sense to Paul, and then again it didn't. Leah was methodical about everything she did. She didn't often react impulsively. The realization that he'd driven her to this desperation was like a nail through his heart.

"Thanks, Jamie, I appreciate the help."

"I'm sorry I wasn't able to tell you more."

"You've helped." She'd given him something to hold on to, and Paul needed that.

"If there's anything I can do, you'll call me back, won't you?"

"Yes," Paul promised.

"Anything," she reminded him.

They spoke for a few minutes longer. Jamie asked if he wanted to talk to Rich, but Paul said no. He was in a rush now, wanting to check the closet. If he could figure out what Leah had taken with her, it might help him discover where she'd gone.

He practically raced into their bedroom, sorting through the closet and drawers. Whatever she'd packed, it hadn't been much. The murder mystery that had been sitting on the nightstand was missing. She planned to go someplace and read? That didn't make sense.

As far as he could figure there weren't any clothes missing. Maybe a pair of jeans and a blouse or two, if that. She hadn't taken her pajamas or her housecoat. Or her toothbrush.

The phone rang just then, and Paul's heart soared to his throat. He walked into the kitchen and reached for the receiver, hoping to catch it before it woke the twins and Kelsey from their naps.

"Hello," he said as calmly as he could, which by his own admission wasn't anything close to sounding composed.

"Paul, it's your father."

"Dad, hello." Paul's mind raced for a reason why his father might be contacting him. Had he heard from Leah?

"Christy had her baby. A little girl. Six pounds, seven ounces. Cute as can be. She's got lots of dark hair, your mother said she would. Christy had heartburn real bad, and Elizabeth claimed that's a sure sign the baby would have a lot of hair and by heaven, she does."

"That's wonderful, Dad. Another granddaughter."

"They've decided to name her Erin Elizabeth. That has a nice sound to it, doesn't it? Naturally your mother's so pleased she's wearing a smile that blinds folks."

"Erin Elizabeth Franklin," Paul repeated.

"Cody's proud as a peacock, as well. He's been handing out cigars to everyone in town."

"Congratulate him and Christy for us, won't you?"

"You bet I will," Eric said enthusiastically. "Taylor says to say hello. She and Russ are going to be adding to their family again in a bit. It's about time if you ask me, but then no one ever did, including your own mother." He chuckled at his own joke.

"Listen, Dad," Paul said casually, not wanting to alert him to his troubles. "I'll contact Jason and Rich and let them know. Do you have any idea when you and Mom will be back to Seattle?"

"You know your mother, she's gonna want to take her time giving this new grandbaby lots of love, but I imagine we'll be back within the next couple of weeks."

"Drive carefully."

"You know I will. Take care, son."

"Thanks, Dad." Paul replaced the receiver.

So Christy and Cody were parents. Despite his current problems, Paul was elated for his sister and brother-in-law. He recalled his own excitement, not so long ago, when Kelsey had been born. His joy had soon been dwarfed by concern for Diane, but those precious moments when he'd heard his daughter's first cries would be held forever in his heart.

He sagged into a kitchen chair, knowing there was nothing he could do until he heard from Leah. He could fret and worry, but it would do little good. He could think back over everything he'd said and list the things he'd done wrong, but that would only depress him further.

Paul was reviewing his options when the front door opened. His heart filled with hope as he moved out of the kitchen and into the living room. He stopped midway into the room as Leah stepped inside, suitcase in hand.

She froze when she saw him. Her eyes were red and puffy, her face so pale he wondered if she might be ill.

"Hello, Paul," she said softly.

Chapter Thirteen

"Leah." Paul stepped toward her, then hesitated, as though he was afraid of saying or doing something more to intimidate her. "Are you all right?"

She nodded, and though she hated herself for being so weak, tears filled her eyes and her throat. "What about you?"

"I'm fine . . . now that you're home."

His gaze fell to the suitcase she was clenching in her hand, and her eyes followed his. She'd forgotten about the bag and was embarrassed now that he'd seen her with it.

Packing her things had been an empty gesture. She'd been distraught, barely aware of what she was doing. All she'd taken with her was a murder mystery and Ryan's yellow blankie. Maybe the five-year-old didn't need his security blanket, but by heaven, she sure did.

Leah hadn't a clue where her mind had been. A book and a blanket! What did she intend to do, curl up under a tree and spend the rest of her life in hiding?

Even more foolish had been her thinking she could leave Paul and the children, for even one night. They were her light, her breath, her substance. It would be easier for her to cut out her own heart than walk away from everything she held so precious.

"I went for a drive," she explained, her voice husky with emotion.

"So did I," Paul said, his own voice so deep and rich it was all she could do not to walk into his arms.

"I...I thought I should get away for a while...clear my head."

"I did the same thing."

No man ever looked as good to her, or sounded as good. Courage bubbled up inside her and she took heart, smiling through her tears. "Did you come up with any solutions?"

Paul's eyes held hers steadily. "The same ones that have been staring me in the face for months. What about you?"

"A few."

"Do you want to talk about them?"

Leah nodded. Paul stepped forward and took the suitcase out of her hand. "I sincerely hope you won't be needing this."

"No...I won't be," she whispered as he set it aside.

Then, taking Leah by the hand, he led her to the sectional and they both sat down. Only a short space separated them, but it seemed to vibrate as if the forces of nature, the forces of their love, were urging them toward each other.

They were silent at first, perhaps afraid of saying the wrong thing, of misunderstanding one another once again. It was all Leah could do not to blurt out everything she'd learned, how much she loved Paul and the children. How serenity had come to her in a cemetery, standing before her sister's burial plot.

"I went to my brother's," Paul spoke first.

"Rich?" Leah had talked to Jamie earlier. She'd tried to hide how upset she was and had done a poor job of it.

"No, Jason. For some unknown reason, I...I found myself outside his apartment," he said, his gaze resting on his hands. "I'm glad I went. Jason didn't say much, not even when I expected he would. Whatever he was thinking, other than to defend you, he kept to himself."

Leah smiled softly. She didn't know him well, but she'd always liked Jason. He seemed like a big, overgrown kid, but beneath the baseball cap was a man with a warm, generous heart.

"Talking helped?" she prodded.

Paul's hands reached for hers. "Yes...I realized what a fool I'd been."

"We've both been fools."

"When Diane died, I never expected to fall in love again," Paul explained. "I didn't think it was possible." He paused as though unsure. "I don't mean to hurt you, by telling you this...."

"You aren't hurting me." She encouraged him with a gentle smile, although emotion was clogging her throat—tears of release and relief.

"I figured a man only finds that kind of love once in his life. Then you came to live with the children and me. In the beginning I was so grateful for your help that I assumed all the feelings I was experiencing toward you had to do with appreciation. I owed you so much.''

"You never understood that I was the one who should be grateful. It was me—"

"You're right," he said, cutting her off. "But I still have trouble believing that. You gave up your life for me.''

"No, I found it instead. If it hadn't been for you and the children, I would have lived all my life teaching the quadratic formula to countless faceless students. I would have grown old without ever knowing what it meant to be in love."

His gaze held hers, then dropped it, as if he had to look away in order to continue. "I don't know if marrying you when I did was the right thing. I was attracted to you. I suspect I was afraid of losing you to Bill Mullins."

"Bill." Leah let loose an abrupt laugh. Paul had no idea of how much she'd come to dislike her colleague. Their last evening together had been a disaster. Bill had tried to pressure her into confessing a sexual relationship with Paul. It seemed beyond his comprehension that the two of them could be living together and not be enjoying an active sex life.

Leah had been insulted and infuriated. She was attracted to Paul and had been for weeks. They'd experienced that one explosive kiss and both had worked hard to avoid repeating the encounter. They'd each been constantly aware of the other's proximity. The sexual tension between them had throbbed every moment they were together.

Bill's innuendos had struck a raw nerve with Leah. She'd barely made it through the evening. The poetry reading had been nearly two hours north of Seattle, and she'd hardly spoken a word on the long drive back. Bill had tried to fill the silence with questions and snatches of conversation, but she'd met his attempts with one-word replies that didn't even dent the strained, stilted silence.

He'd grown impatient with her, and by the time they'd reached Paul's house, he was angry and demanding. Leah had practically leapt out of his car, announcing she wanted nothing more to do with him and escaping inside before he had a chance to argue or delay her. She hadn't heard from him since and, frankly, she was grateful.

"I was jealous of Bill," Paul confessed. "And I hated myself for it... because it made me aware of several things I wasn't ready to face. First and foremost, I was feeling again.

"For months my emotions had been desensitized. Anything I did feel only scratched the surface of my senses. There were times I laughed, but I was never happy. There were times I looked forward to another day, but I wasn't whole. I wasn't at peace with myself. Six months after Diane's death and I was still clinging to her, holding on to her with both hands, deathly afraid of what would happen if I were to ever let her go."

"When your parents suggested we marry, I was stunned." Leah had her own confessions to make. "I didn't think you'd want to marry anyone like me...."

"Why not?"

All the old doubts and fears had come back to plague her. All the insecurities of her youth. "I'm not... Diane."

"No, you're Leah. Warm, beautiful, gentle Leah."

Leah didn't feel she possessed any of those qualities, until she'd fallen in love with Paul. "I was afraid."

"But why?" Paul wanted to know, looking bewildered.

"I was convinced that sometime down the road, a year from now, or even sooner, you'd wake up and realize you were saddled with me and—"

"Saddled with you? Leah, for the love of heaven..."

"Please, listen." She couldn't allow him to distract her from addressing her fears. "I'm not beautiful, I'm plain. I've known it all my life, and I've accepted it." She paused when it looked as though Paul were going to protest again. Pressing the tips of her fingers across his lips, she continued, "I don't possess a gregarious personality. I couldn't change who I am, not even to please you. When I agreed to marry you, I did so for purely selfish reasons."

"Leah—"

Once more she stopped him. "I did so because I couldn't bear to leave the children and because... because I was falling in love with you, and it frightened me to death. For the first time in my life I had a chance at finding what had always escaped me. A husband, a family, people who loved me, and I grabbed hold of it with both hands, damning the consequences."

"Our marriage was grossly unfair to you."

"Don't you understand?" she cried. "*I* was taking advantage of *you*. I knew the time would come when you'd regret marrying me, yet I went ahead with it anyway."

"Leah, I'm never going to regret marrying you."

"Maybe you should."

"No." He vaulted upright and moved away from her, walking to the window and looking out. "I'm not entirely sure when it happened, but I discovered I loved you as deeply and as profoundly as I've ever loved in my life."

"And I...I discovered what it meant to love through you and the children." Leah's voice was soft and dreamy.

Paul turned toward her then and continued. "I expected to feel guilty for loving you and fulfilled the prophecy. Only, to my surprise, I had to force myself to feel the guilt. Any time I analyzed my feelings for you, I realized loving you was what Diane would have wanted. But I dared not admit it, because that would mean releasing Diane, and I wasn't ready to do that.

"I was caught between the two of you. Standing between two worlds. Trapped between yesterday and tomorrow. The more time I spent with you, the dimmer my vision of Diane became, and that frightened me. Yet I couldn't make myself stop loving you." He looked away from her. "I embarrassed myself with how often I needed to make love to you."

"I...wanted you, too."

"I was never as demanding with Diane—don't misunderstand me, we had a healthy sex life—but I wasn't the fiend I've been with you."

"I don't believe you ever heard me complain."

"I couldn't understand myself. I wanted you so much, yet every time we made love I felt as though I were being unfaithful to Diane's memory. At the same time I feared I was cheating you, not being the type of husband I should have been. It was confusing the hell out of me, and yet there I was, night after night, so eager to get you into bed I could barely wait for the kids to go down."

"Until you thought I might be pregnant...then you couldn't bear to touch me." Leah lowered her eyes because the pain was still there, and she didn't want him to know how badly she'd been hurt.

"No." Paul covered the distance between them in three giant strides. He sat next to her and reached for her hands. "It wasn't that, Leah. It wasn't anything like that. I don't think I've ever known a greater fear than when you told me you might be pregnant. The thought of losing you terrified me. I think I went a little crazy. I knew my attitude hurt you, and I'm sorry, so very sorry."

He pressed his forehead against hers, and his voice roughened. "It was when you thought you might be pregnant that I came to realize how much I really loved you. It hit me on the head like a baseball bat."

As if to rub away the pain he'd inflicted, Paul's arms came around her. "I was left to face my greatest fear. Losing the woman I loved. Now, looking back, I realize how badly I behaved, how much my attitude hurt you. I'm sorry for that, sorrier than you'll ever know."

"You were so angry."

"But never with you. If there was anyone I blamed, it was myself. At the same time I was forced to own up to how much I loved you, and how much I loved Diane. I didn't know it was possible to love two women at the same time...then it came to me—I didn't."

Was this the realization he'd come to when he had talked to his brother? Leah wondered. Her heart started to pound louder and louder, harder and harder.

"Friday night . . ."

She pulled her hands free from his and lowered her gaze. Their lovemaking the night before had been beautiful. Just thinking about it brought tears to her eyes. Remembering how Paul had held her in his arms afterward, teased her, laughed with her. He had made her feel more wanted and loved in one evening than she'd felt in her entire life. She'd gone to sleep content, having experienced a joy that went beyond words. A joy that radiated from the furthest reaches of her dark, lonely soul.

Then she'd woken to the sound of another woman's name on her husband's lips.

"That night," Paul continued, "was one of the most beautiful experiences I've ever known. Yes, the lovemaking was incredible, but it always had been. You went to sleep in my arms, and as I lay there I realized what was different, what had changed." He tucked his finger under her chin and raised her face until her eyes locked with his. "I realized Friday night that I'd released Diane. I'd let go of her and stepped out of yesterday and into today, tomorrow . . . my life with you."

"But you called me Diane."

"I had a dream," Paul said, his words heavy with regret. "I can't explain it, nor can I make excuses for it, but . . . in my dream Diane was there. I can't remember exactly what happened, just bits and snatches.

"Jason seems to think my subconscious had something to do with it. He theorized that Diane was releasing me, too. I don't know what it was, or if any of this makes sense to you. I can't promise I won't dream about her again, but in my heart I don't believe I will. It's over. I'm at peace about her death, at peace with myself. It didn't come easy, and it took far longer than it should have." He hesitated then, as though waiting for a reaction from her.

"Diane came to me in a dream once, too," Leah told him. It was the first time she'd ever told anyone about the experience that night.

"This Friday?"

"No, no... the night she died. I was exhausted and I was certain my mind was playing tricks on me. She looked so happy, I couldn't understand it. She was sitting under a tree with wildflowers all around her."

"What kind of flowers?"

His question seemed odd to Leah. "I don't remember, except she was holding a—"

"A daisy."

"Yes." Her eyes widened with surprise. "How'd you know?"

"In my dream she was sitting under a tree, that much I remember. She seemed so happy, plucking the petals from a yellow daisy."

"Yes!" Leah flattened her hand over her heart. "Yes," she repeated. "There was a light, too."

"Brilliant and white?"

"Yes." Once more Leah nodded.

"What did she say?" Paul asked her.

"She told me she was going away. I tried to argue with her, tried to make her stay, but she didn't have time to listen to me. She said she had to get us away from the hospital because we were holding her back.

And then...then she explained that she had to go away, that she hadn't wanted to in the beginning, but had come to understand it would be all right for her to leave. She...she asked me if I'd take her place."

"Take her place?"

Leah nodded. "I didn't understand what she meant, but I didn't question her, either. She looked right at me. I'd never been able to refuse Diane before, and so I promised her I would."

Paul was silent for a moment. "I don't remember what she said to me, but I think Jason might be right. I think she did come to say goodbye."

They grew silent, each mulling over the similarities of their experiences, each lost in the memory of the one they'd loved so much.

"It was because of the dream that I decided to come live with you, but I never intended on falling in love with you," Leah confessed. "You talk about experiencing guilt and about being trapped between two worlds...in many ways that's how I felt, too. I was afraid to love you, fighting it, but at the same time I'd never been happier, never felt more fulfilled."

She didn't know how to put into words all that was in her heart. How could she explain that she belonged to him in ways she didn't even belong to herself?

"You felt guilty?"

Leah grinned sheepishly. "When I left today, I...I went for a drive and ended up at the cemetery. I hadn't been out there since the funeral. I wasn't even sure where her burial plot was. It took me a long time to find it, and when I did I just stood there, not knowing what to say, but knowing I had to say something."

"I haven't been out there in weeks." Paul's voice was low and incredulous, as though he'd only just realized as much. "The need to talk to her left me after we married."

Leah continued. "I didn't know what to say... or even why I was there. I told her how well the twins and Kelsey were doing, and then I got angry. I so seldom raise my voice that I think I frightened myself. I hated what was happening to me. Hated competing with her when I'd never wanted to compete before. For the first time in my life I wanted something she had, and I didn't know how to handle it."

"Oh, Leah..." His thumb caressed the softness of her cheek. Leah closed her eyes, loving the glorious feel of his skin touching hers.

"I shouted at her, demanding to know if this was what she wanted... for me to love you. Because it was killing me—loving you, when you loved her. I was jealous as I'd never been before, not once in all the years we grew up together."

Paul brought her into his arms, adjusting their positions so she was cradled in his embrace, her head resting against the solid strength of his chest.

"Did you find any answers?"

"Yes." A smile came over her, one that radiated out from her heart. "I was standing there, weeping, knowing I was asking the impossible, demanding an answer, when there was none to be given. Only there was."

"But how... what answer?"

"It had been drizzling most of the morning. The sky had been dark and overcast."

"Yes," Paul concurred.

"As I was standing there, the sun broke through the clouds. I watched as the sky parted and this brilliant stream of light shot down and dappled the earth." Leah wasn't sure she should have continued, whether Paul would believe her or not. The sun parting the sky wasn't God writing out the Ten Commandments, or a spectacular miracle; it was an everyday phenomenon. An everyday kind of miracle.

"In my heart I had my answer," Leah whispered, close to tears. "You and the children are Diane's gift to me. She gave me what she loved the most...you four. She knows me so well. All along she realized I was going to fall in love with you...it was what she wanted."

"She knew I would love you, too," Paul added. "That we'd both fight it because of our loyalty to her, and yet, if she'd been able, she would have told us our love was by design. Her own design."

"She loved us both so much."

"Loves," Paul corrected softly, tightening his embrace. "I don't think that will ever change." His arms were holding her close when Leah sensed they were no longer alone.

Slowly she opened her eyes and turned toward the hallway. Ryan stood there, rubbing the sleep from his eyes. As she watched the child—her child—her heart swelled with love.

"Did you sleep good, sweetheart?" she asked.

Ryan nodded. "Kindergartners are too old for naps."

It was a point he argued loud and often, and yet the five-year-old fell asleep of his own accord each afternoon.

"I'm too old for naps, too," Ronnie announced, appearing by his brother's side and yawning loudly. "Only babies go to bed in the afternoon."

"I'd give a good deal to be in bed right now," Paul whispered in Leah's ear. "You wouldn't hear me complaining about taking a nap, if you'd take one with me."

"Paul," she chastised softly.

"Come here, boys," Paul urged his sons. They scooted into their father's lap and all three snuggled together while Leah went to check on Kelsey. If the boys were awake, then it was likely their sister was up, too.

Sure enough, the toddler was standing in her crib, her chubby legs bouncing as she danced back and forth. She broke into a wide grin when she saw Leah.

"How's my sweetheart?" Leah asked, holding out her hands.

Kelsey raised her arms to Leah and delivered a sentence or two of happy gibberish.

Leah and Kelsey joined Paul and the boys, and the five of them sat together on the sofa—Paul holding the twins, and Leah holding Kelsey. They'd come together, the five of them, and Leah realized they were a family. One formed in love. A gift she'd received from her sister. The gift of love.

Love...it was more than she'd dared to dream. More than she'd ever thought to have.

Love had found a place for her.

Paul's eyes searched out hers and he smiled.

Leah smiled, too. She felt his love, in his smile, in his touch, in the warm gentle look in his eyes.

For Leah and Paul, it was only the beginning.

* * * * *

COMING NEXT MONTH

FREE GIFT OFFER

To receive your free gift, send us the specified number of proofs-of-purchase from any specially marked Free Gift Offer Harlequin or Silhouette book with the Free Gift Certificate properly completed, plus a check or money order (do not send cash) to cover postage and handling payable to Harlequin/Silhouette Free Gift Promotion Offer. We will send you the specified gift.

FREE GIFT CERTIFICATE

ITEM	A. GOLD TONE EARRINGS	B. GOLD TONE BRACELET	C. GOLD TONE NECKLACE
# of proofs-of-purchase required	3	6	9
Postage and Handling	$2.25	$2.75	$3.25
Check one	☐	☐	☐

Name: _____

Address: _____

City: _____ Province: _____ Postal Code: _____

Mail this certificate, specified number of proofs-of-purchase and a check or money order for postage and handling to: HARLEQUIN/SILHOUETTE FREE GIFT OFFER 1992, P.O. Box 622, Fort Erie, Ontario L2A 5X3. Requests must be received by July 31, 1992.

PLUS—Every time you submit a completed certificate with the correct number of proofs-of-purchase, you are automatically entered in our MILLION DOLLAR SWEEPSTAKES! No purchase or obligation necessary to enter. See below for alternate means of entry and how to obtain complete sweepstakes rules.

✂ SS2C

ONE PROOF-OF-PURCHASE
To collect your fabulous FREE GIFT you must include the necessary FREE GIFT proofs-of-purchase with a properly completed offer certificate.

(See inside back cover for offer details)